LOVE RULES

"I cannot...bear it!" Paulina protested. "I am not...strong like...you. I want to be with you...to see you...to love you."

Prince Maximus laid his cheek against hers. "I shall think of you, dream of you, and wherever I am, I shall feel somehow that you are near me."

"I shall...feel that...too," Paulina replied. "However long we may be...parted...I somehow feel...one day we shall be...together."

Then his lips came down on hers.

She reverberated to the wonder of his kiss and felt the sunshine pass through her body and from her lips to his.

Suddenly he took his arms from her, moved away and disappeared through the thick shrubs.

The rapture he had aroused in her body battled with her mind and forced her to face the truth that he was gone. Then the tears came. Slowly, agonizingly, they crept down her cheeks and she felt as if each one were a drop of blood from her heart.

Bantam Books by Barbara Cartland
Ask your bookseller for the books you have missed

126	LUCIFER AND THE ANGEL
127	OLA AND THE SEA WOLF
128	THE PRUDE AND THE PRODICAL
129	LOVE FOR SALE
130	THE GODDESS AND THE GAIETY GIRL
131	SIGNPOST TO LOVE
132	LOST LAUGHTER
133	FROM HELL TO HEAVEN
134	PRIDE AND THE POOR PRINCESS
135	THE LIONESS AND THE LILY
138	LOVE IN THE MOON
139	THE WALTZ OF HEARTS
141	DREAMS DO COME TRUE
143	ENCHANTED
144	WINGED MAGIC
145	A PORTRAIT OF LOVE
146	THE RIVER OF LOVE
147	GIFT OF THE GODS
148	AN INNOCENT IN RUSSIA
149	A SHAFT OF SUNLIGHT
150	LOVE WINS
151	SECRET HARBOUR
152	LOOKING FOR LOVE
153	THE VIBRATIONS OF LOVE
154	LIES FOR LOVE
155	LOVE RULES

Love Rules

Barbara Cartland

BANTAM BOOKS
TORONTO · NEW YORK · LONDON · SYDNEY

LOVE RULES
A Bantam Book / April 1982

ISBN 0-553-20948-5

Published simultaneously in the United States and Canada

Bantam Books are published by Bantam Books, Inc. Its trademark, consisting of the words "Bantam Books" and the portrayal of a rooster, is Registered in U. S. Patent and Trademark Office and in other countries. Marca Registrada. Bantam Books, Inc., 666 Fifth Avenue, New York, New York 10103.

PRINTED IN THE UNITED STATES OF AMERICA

0 9 8 7 6 5 4 3 2 1

Author's Note

Shamyl, Imam of Dagestan, fought against the invading Russians in a terrible bloody war which lasted from 1804 to 1861.

In one battle he lost his precious Koran and it was picked up on the battlefield by Prince Alexander of Hesse. When I held it in my hands, I felt as if I had stepped into a momentous and thrilling piece of history.

The hero in this story follows in some particulars the dramatic romance of Prince Alexander's elopement and marriage, which began the famous Royal Line of Battenburg to Mountbatten.

Chapter One

Paulina, driving in a carriage over the dusty roads towards the Palace, wondered why Princess Margarita had sent for her.

They were great friends and were continually together, but as she had seen the Princess only yesterday it seemed strange to receive such an urgent summons to visit her again today.

Ever since Sir Christopher Handley had been appointed Minister to the small Royal Duchy of Altauss, Paulina had been extremely grateful that the Grand Duke Louis's daughter was the same age as herself.

Her father had been so depressed at being posted to Altauss that Paulina had expected to find herself isolated in a dull and regimented country and with no friends.

Instead, from the moment she had seen Altauss she had thought how pretty it was with its high mountains bordered on one side by Prussia and on the others by Saxony and Austria.

What was more, the people of Altauss were charming, good-natured, and apparently very content with their Ruler, the Grand Duke.

This was something that both Paulina and even more so her father had not expected.

"We are being exiled to the back of beyond!" he had grumbled. "We shall have to do nothing but bow and curtsey to a set of stiff-necked and disagreeable

1

minor Royalty, who will think they are God Almighty and are detested by the populace over whom they rule."

Paulina, who loved her father, was both sorry for him and very understanding in regard to the predicament in which he had landed them both.

The fact was, as she had told herself before, her father could not help being so handsome that he was irresistible to women, so that wherever he went there was always a chance of his *affaires de coeur* causing gossip and scandal, which was frowned on by the Foreign Office in England.

Sir Christopher, who had been Number Two to the Minister in Rome, had hoped that he would be appointed Ambassador to Paris.

Unfortunately, a very beautiful and alluring Italian *Contessa* had proved irresistible, and her husband had not only challenged Sir Christopher to a duel but had caused so much trouble in diplomatic circles that he had to be posted to a more obscure part of Europe.

It was distressing that, after so many tempestuous and fiery love-affairs, when approaching the pinnacle of his career he should be punished for what he considered a very minor crime.

He was in fact so depressed that Paulina found it hard to comfort him, thinking as she had thought so often before that none of this would have happened if her mother had not died.

She had never known two people so happy and so much in love with each other as her parents had been, and when her mother had been carried off by a fever within a week, she had thought that her father would never recover from the blow.

At first he had seemed but a shadow of his usually buoyant self. Then, when another man might have turned to drink for consolation, Sir Christopher had allowed the lovely women who had always before pursued him hopelessly to try to make him forget with the softness of their arms and lips.

Paulina, brought up in the cosmopolitan atmosphere which was inevitable for a Diplomat's daughter, had understood and known that no woman could take the place of her mother, whom he had really loved.

But to be posted to the Grand Duchy of Altauss had been, as far as Sir Christopher was concerned, to move into exile and was as depressing as being sent to Siberia.

However, Paulina discovered that it was no punishment for her father when he found that the Grand Duke Louis was an intelligent man with a sense of humour, and the nobles who surrounded him were not only sportsmen, hard riders, and excellent shots, but were as cultured as he was.

While Sir Christopher quickly made a number of friends, Princess Margarita offered Paulina a closer friendship than any she had ever had in any other country in which they had lived.

The Princess was very pretty, with dark hair, sparkling eyes, and a grace which came from her Polish mother, while her expertise as a horsewoman was undoubtedly inherited from her Hungarian grandmother, and Paulina admired her wholeheartedly.

They also had a bond in common in that Paulina's mother had Hungarian blood in her veins, which accounted for the fact that she too could ride in a way which evoked the admiration of every man who saw her and the envy of every woman.

Because Paulina had travelled with her father since she was small she had become fluent in many languages.

As Princess Margarita had the same proficiency, they talked with each other in French or Italian, German or Russian, thinking it amusing that other people present understood little of what they were saying.

In fact, the Princess would often say something

outrageous just to make Paulina laugh, and Paulina would say to her afterwards:

"You must please be careful, Your Royal Highness! You know as well as I do that if your Statesmen think I am laughing at them, I shall be in as much disgrace at home as poor Papa is at the moment."

"I do not believe your father could be in disgrace with anybody!" the Princess replied. "He is so handsome and so charming that whatever crimes he committed, he would undoubtedly be forgiven immediately."

That might be true, Paulina thought wryly, if the Foreign Office consisted of women rather than stern, disapproving men who took a very serious view of the complaints that reached them from Europe.

Yet, after five months in Altauss, Paulina was beginning to hope that the reports wending their way by devious routes back to Whitehall would be so complimentary about her father that any past sins would soon be committed to the archives and forgotten.

At the same time, she personally was in no hurry to leave Altauss.

There were plenty of tall, handsome young men with whom to dance, there were picnic-parties in the foot-hills of the mountains, and now that the weather was growing warmer she was sure that, although it seemed very daring, she and the Princess might be allowed to swim in one of the numerous beautiful lakes with which the country abounded.

"I like being here," Paulina told herself as the horses moved swiftly despite the fact that the ground rose sharply as it led up to the Palace.

It was a fairy-tale building, standing high above the valley which was filled with the pink and white blossoms of the fruit trees and the alpine flowers which grew in profusion at this time of the year.

Looking up at the blue sky above the Palace, Paulina was not aware that the blue was reflected in her eyes.

She took after her father in colouring.

Her hair was the pale gold of ripening corn, her skin was translucently pink and white, and her eyes, which seemed to fill her small, heart-shaped face, were fringed with long lashes which were dark at the base and tipped with gold.

Sometimes those who admired her thought she looked like a lovable and very young child, but she was too intelligent to leave this impression in anybody's mind for long.

There was also something very attractive in the way her expression would become mischievous and two provocative little dimples would appear at the sides of her mouth.

"You have a naughty face!" the Princess had said once.

"I hope not," Paulina replied, "and I think it is unkind of you to say so."

"I do not mean wicked," the Princess protested, "I just mean that you look as if you might be up to mischief of some sort. It is really very alluring."

Paulina had laughed, and she knew that the Italians in Rome who paid her fulsome compliments had said much the same thing.

"I think you are an angel in front of whom I should kneel and burn candles," one of the young men had said. "But when you laugh at me, I know you are a little demon sent from hell to torment me!"

Paulina had laughed at him again, but she remembered that her Nanny had always said that everybody had two sides to their character.

"There's an angel sitting on your right shoulder," she had said when Paulina was old enough to understand, "and a little devil sitting on your left. They are both whispering in your ear, and it's up to you as to which one you listen to."

Paulina had often sat quietly listening to what the "angel" and the "little devil" were saying to her, and she had the suspicion that what the "little devil" said was more exciting!

The carriage had reached the great ornamental gates of the Palace, and the sentries standing outside their boxes, which had been painted with pink and white stripes, presented arms.

Paulina had seen them often and she now bent forward to wave her hand and smile, recognizing the two young soldiers who were on guard duty and thinking how smart they looked in their red and white uniforms.

She was met at the door of the Palace by a servant who led her through the impressive Hall, with its statues of former Grand Dukes and portraits of their plump Duchesses, up the red-carpeted staircase, and and along a wide corridor to the Princess's rooms.

Paulina, who had been there so many times before, could quite easily have found her own way.

But she knew that to suggest such a thing would offend the protocol of the Palace, and the servants would not understand why she should wish to dispense with their services.

Accordingly, because she had to follow a fat, middle-aged man-servant with his white wig causing beads of sweat on his forehead, she had to move a great deal more slowly than she would have done had she been alone.

But at last they reached the apartments in the West Wing which were the Princess Margarita's, and the man-servant knocked on a large door painted artistically with the wild flowers of the district on a background of peacock blue.

It was opened by one of the Princess's maids, who dropped Paulina a small curtsey.

"It is good to see you, gracious *Fraulein*," she said. "Her Royal Highness has been asking over and over again how it is possible for you to take so long in coming to her."

"Long?" Paulina queried. "I came immediately I received Her Royal Highness's note, and the horses moved as if they had wings on their feet."

"That is what we'll all need before we are finished," the maid said almost beneath her breath.

She opened a door and announced:

"*Fraulein* Paulina Handley, Your Royal Highness!"

With a cry of delight the Princess sprang up from the chair in which she had been sitting, upsetting a large number of articles that had been in her lap as she did so.

"Paulina! Thank goodness you have come!" she exclaimed in English. "I began to think you had deserted me."

"Deserted you?" Paulina exclaimed in surprise. "Why should I do that?"

"I had to see you! I have so much to tell you, and you must help me."

The maid had closed the door behind her and they were alone, and the Princess took Paulina's hand and pulled her towards the sofa.

"What do you think has happened?" she asked.

"I cannot imagine."

The Princess drew in a deep breath.

"I am to be married!"

This was certainly not what Paulina had expected, and she looked at her friend in astonishment.

"But . . . to whom?"

As she spoke she thought of all the young men who had been in attendance at the Balls and could not imagine that any of them would be particularly suitable husbands for the Princess Margarita, however well they might qualify as dancing-partners.

The Princess did not reply for a moment, then holding Paulina's hand tightly in hers she said:

"Will you promise me on everything you hold sacred that you will do what I ask?"

Paulina smiled.

"I cannot promise that unless I know what you want me to do."

"It is quite simple," the Princess replied. "I want you to come with me to Russia."

Paulina stared at her in astonishment.

"To Russia?" she echoed. "But why... what has ... happened? Can you be going to ... marry a Russian?"

The Princess nodded her head.

"Papa told me last night," she said. "Oh, Paulina, it is thrilling in some ways, but at the same time I am frightened. Frightened of going so far away from Papa and also of being alone in a strange country."

Paulina covered her hand with hers.

"Start from the beginning," she begged. "I cannot understand at all what has happened."

"You cannot be more bewildered than I am."

The Princess paused and drew in a long breath before she began:

"Last night after you left, Papa sent for me. I could see from the moment I entered the room that he was very delighted about something, but I never suspected I never... had the ... slightest idea of what it ... might be."

Paulina said nothing. She was merely thinking how pretty Margarita looked, even though her lovely eyes were dark with apprehension and there was no smile on her full lips.

"It was then," she went on, "that Papa told me what had happened."

"And what was that?"

"You will remember I told you that my brother Maximus has been in Russia for some years?"

"Yes, you told me that," Paulina replied, "and that the Grand Duke had received an invitation from the Tsar for him to live at the Court and serve in the Russian Imperial Army."

Although Paulina had heard the story many times,

she had never met Prince Maximus, so she had not
been particularly interested.

"The Tsar is very pleased with Maximus," Princess
Margarita went on in a low voice, "so pleased that he
has promoted him to the rank of Major-General, because he has won great glory in the war in the Caucasus."

"Your father must be delighted!" Paulina exclaimed.

She knew how proud the Grand Duke was of his
only son, and that he had distinguished himself in battle
would delight the whole of the Duchy.

"Yes, Papa is very excited," the Princess agreed,
"but in the same letter in which Maximus wrote that he
had won the Order of St. George in battle, he said that
the Tsar had agreed that I should marry his cousin, the
Grand Duke Vladirvitch."

Paulina's eyes widened.

She was a little vague about the hierarchy in the
Russian Court, but her upbringing in the Diplomatic
Service had taught her that the position of Grand Duke
was a very important one, and to be a cousin of the Tsar
carried in itself enormous prestige.

Even so, Paulina felt that happiness in marriage
was far more important than a title, however grand.

"Have you met the Grand Duke?" she asked.

"Just once," Princess Margarita replied, "but the
trouble is, Paulina, I cannot remember what he was
like. He came here for a short visit and the Palace was
filled with relations from all over Europe to celebrate
Mama and Papa's twenty-fifth Wedding Anniversary."

For the first time she smiled as she went on:

"The Emperor of Austria had a very attractive
Aide-de-Camp, and as I was talking to him and dancing
as many times with him as I dared, I did not notice the
other guests."

"The Grand Duke certainly must have remembered
you!"

"That is what Maximus says, and not only does he

want to marry me, but the Tsar has given his permission.

"Oh, dearest, I can only hope that you will be very, very happy!" Paulina cried.

"But Russia is so far away," the Princess complained, "and I will only contemplate going there if you will come with me."

"But how can I? Will they not think it strange . . . ?" Paulina began.

"You will come as my Lady-in-Waiting," the Princess interposed. "I am certainly not going to take that boring old Baroness Schwaez with me, and I doubt if she would come anyway. She has a large family and is always complaining of how unhappy she is to be away from them."

"I do not . . . think Papa will . . . let me go," Paulina said hesitatingly.

"If I explain to Sir Christopher how much I need you, and that I promise not to keep you for a very long time, I am sure he will understand," the Princess said. "Oh, please, please, Paulina, you cannot desert me now when I need you so terribly."

Paulina was touched by the appeal in her voice.

Nobody knew better than she did how sensitive Princess Margarita was about many things and that it would be a great strain on her to have to live away from her own country, and in Russia of all places.

The stories about Russia, while intriguing, were also rather frightening, and the tales about Tsar Nicholas grew more and more macabre.

Paulina thought she could think of nothing more terrifying than to be married to a Russian and live under the edict of a Ruler whom even the most diplomatic of Diplomats described amongst themselves as both "eccentric and tyrannical."

However, because she loved Margarita and wanted her to be happy, Paulina knew that in no circumstances would she ever repeat such opinions to her.

She was wise enough to understand that the Princess was being offered a position that from a worldly point of view exceeded anything that the Grand Duke Louis could have hoped for or desired for his daughter.

Whatever the Princess might feel, she would be married to the Grand Duke and therefore must accept the situation whether or not it fulfilled her dreams.

Because she knew it was the right thing to do, Paulina said:

"I think you are very, very, lucky, and I am sure you will be extremely happy with the Grand Duke."

"In Russia?" the Princess queried.

"Why not?" Paulina asked. "And as it is now so much easier and quicker to travel by train, I expect your husband will take you to Paris, London, and undoubtedly the South of France."

"Papa was saying the other day that the Russian Aristocrats enjoy France because it is so gay," the Princess remarked, "but he never mentioned that their wives went with them."

This was a problem for which Paulina had no answer, and she said quickly:

"The Tsar and his family are enormously wealthy, so you will live in great grandeur."

"I shall be very important at Court," the Princess said as if she spoke to herself.

"Of course you will," Paulina agreed, "and Papa says Russian Aristocrats have the most fabulous jewels in the whole world, so you will look very beautiful at the Balls which are given at the Winter Palace."

Some of the anxiety seemed to fade from the Princess's face. Then she said quickly:

"I refuse to go unless you say you will come with me."

"I shall have to talk to Papa before I can promise you that," Paulina replied.

"I will ask my father to speak to him too," the Princess said. "You never know, if the Tsar takes a fancy to you he might ask that Sir Christopher be appointed as British Ambassador to St. Petersburg!"

Paulina laughed.

"I can see that before you are finished, all your friends will somehow find their way to the Imperial Court!"

"Why not?" Princess Margarita asked. "If I am going to be so grand, I might as well have what I want, and I want you, dearest Paulina, far more than I want diamonds and emeralds."

As the Princess was speaking, Paulina realized that she was gradually becoming used to the idea of leaving her home and living in Russia, and they talked of what it would be like, exchanging their limited knowledge of a country they had neither of them ever seen.

When it was time for Paulina to leave and drive back to her father, the Princess pleaded with her.

"Promise, promise that you will not fail me," she begged, "for even though Maximus will be in St. Petersburg, it will not be the same as having you there. No man could ever understand how frightened I feel of marrying someone I cannot even remember."

Paulina thought that she also would be very frightened in the same position.

But she knew that Royal marriages were always arranged, and there was no question that if it was something the Tsar had decreed, Princess Margarita would be unable to refuse.

At the same time, as she drove back in the carriage she thought how lucky she was to be a commoner.

Her father and mother had married because they loved each other, and that was why they had been so happy.

"When I marry somebody it will be because I love him, and it will not matter whether we live in a Palace or a cottage as long as we are together," she told herself.

Paulina had lived too long in diplomatic circles not

to realize that such a freedom of choice was only for those of no social consequence and certainly not for anybody who had Royal blood.

It was true that the Grand Duke Vladirvitch was thirty-five and Margarita only eighteen, but she knew that the Princess might easily have been chosen as the bride of a man who was very much older and perhaps desperate for an heir before he died.

"Arranged marriages are a hideous idea," she told herself.

She knew that very few people would agree, but to her it seemed criminal that regardless of any human feelings Royal blood must be espoused to Royal blood and a nobleman must marry a woman of noble birth.

"Perhaps in complete contrast I shall fall in love with a crossing-sweeper," Paulina said to herself with a little smile, "or perhaps an ordinary soldier with nothing to recommend him except his smart uniform."

This thought came to her as she saw the sentries outside the British Ministry who presented arms as her carriage drew up outside the front door, which was surmounted by a Union Jack.

Paulina jumped out and ran into the house.

"Where is His Excellency?" she asked of the servants in the Hall.

"In the Study, Miss."

Paulina ran down the passage and burst into the Study, hoping as she did so that her father would be alone.

She was fortunate.

Sir Christopher was sitting comfortably in a deep leather armchair with a newspaper on his knees, although his head was laid back against a cushion and his eyes were closed.

"Papa, wake up, Papa!" Paulina cried as she ran towards him.

"Hello, my dear," Sir Christopher replied in a drowsy voice. "I must have dropped off."

Paulina took off her bonnet and flung it down in a chair, then knelt down beside her father, her full skirts billowing round her.

"Listen, Papa, listen!"

Sir Christopher's eyes were on her face as she spoke, and he thought with a pang in his heart that his daughter was very like her mother.

Only to think of his wife, whom he had loved so deeply, was to bring back the agony of losing her, and he put out his hand to Paulina as if he would hold her close and never let her go.

"I have just been to the Palace, Papa," Paulina said, "and what do you think has happened?"

Sir Christopher smiled.

"The Grand Duke Vladirvitch has proposed marriage!"

"Oh, you knew!" Paulina exclaimed.

"The Prime Minister told me as I was leaving after a conference we had this afternoon. It is a great honour, not only for the Grand Duke but for the whole Duchy."

"And you think Margarita will be happy?" Paulina asked.

Her father shrugged his shoulders.

"We can only hope so, for there is no reason to believe that Vladirvitch resembles his cousin the Tsar— at least we hope not, for your friend's sake."

Paulina drew in her breath.

"The Princess says she will not go to Russia unless I can go with her!"

Sir Christopher stiffened.

"What are you saying?"

"She has begged me to be her Lady-in-Waiting. She refuses categorically to take the Baroness, and she has to have somebody."

"But why you?"

"She trusts me, and I think she loves me."

There was a far-away look in Sir Christopher's eyes as he said:

"This is certainly something I did not expect."

"Neither did I," Paulina agreed. "I could not imagine why the Princess was sending so urgently for me when I was at the Palace only yesterday."

There was silence. Then after a moment she went on:

"You know I have no wish to leave you, Papa, but the Princess is very insistent that she will not go without me, although of course she can be forced to do so. But I think it would hardly augur well for her to arrive in St. Petersburg in chains!"

"I agree," Sir Christopher said.

After a moment's thought he added:

"In a way it might be interesting and educational for you to visit Russia."

Paulina smiled.

"Princess Margarita is sure she will be able to persuade the Tsar to ask for you to come to St. Petersburg as the British Ambassador!"

Sir Christopher laughed.

"I think that is very unlikely while I am still in disgrace, but you never know how things will work out."

"Can I tell her I may go, Papa?"

"I will not urge you to do so if you dislike the idea," Sir Christopher replied. "At the same time, if your visit is limited to a few months, I must try to manage without you."

"But you will miss me, Papa?"

"Of course, my dearest child. You know how much you mean to me. I shall be very lonely when you are gone."

Paulina smiled.

"I think you will find there are plenty of lovely ladies only too eager to console you. In fact, I was wondering when I came into the study whether the Baroness von Butzweil would be here looking up at you adoringly."

Father and daughter both laughed.

"She is certainly very beautiful," Paulina said, "although I think she is not as good-natured and as kindly as the *Contesse* Valmaro."

Sir Christopher put back his head and laughed.

"Instead of you choosing suitable women for me," he said, "I should be choosing eligible suitors for you!"

"I am only pointing out that you will not be lonely without me," Paulina said, "while I, on the other hand, will miss you desperately, Papa. You must promise me that if I do go you will stipulate that I must return at the end of two or perhaps three months at most, like a parcel, intact and undamaged."

Sir Christopher laughed again.

"You can be quite sure of that, and quite frankly I think three months is a long time."

"It would be so for me, Papa," Paulina said softly, "so make it clear that you will give your permission for me to accompany the Princess only on condition that I am back here in July."

"If you overstay, I shall come and fetch you myself!" Sir Christopher promised.

Paulina put her arms round his neck.

"I love you, Papa, I love being with you, but I am also very fond of the Princess, and I have a feeling that it is my duty to try to make her happy."

"I think only a husband can do that," Sir Christopher said drily. "At the same time, you can certainly dispel some of her shyness and her quite understandable apprehension at becoming a member of the Tsar's family."

"Is he really so ferocious and awe-inspiring?"

"I am afraid a great number of the stories about him are too fantastic to have been invented," Sir Christopher replied, "but there is no doubt that he is a devoted family man, as Princess Margarita will discover when she joins the family."

"That is certainly a saving grace," Paulina said with a smile.

"Try to keep her from hearing the more unpleasant stories about His Imperial Majesty," Sir Christopher ordered.

"I will do my best," Paulina said, "but there will always be people who will think she *'ought to know'* the worst and will assure her that is what she will encounter."

"I would like to tell them to hold their tongues!" Sir Christopher said sharply. "But you are quite right, my darling, to try to make the future seem for her as happy as possible. God knows, it is all too easy to be disillusioned in life."

Paulina slipped her hand into his.

"I was thinking when I was coming back home, Papa, that when I marry I want it to be because I am in love, so that I shall be as happy as you and Mama always were."

"That is what I pray will happen to you," Sir Christopher replied, "but make no mistake, dearest child, it is not easy in these difficult and turbulent times to find the right person who is the other half of one's self."

"That is how I always thought you and Mama were," Paulina said. "You complemented each other. Mama was so soft, sweet, and feminine, and you so strong and masculine."

"I worshipped her," Sir Christopher said in a low voice, "and nothing and nobody could ever take her place. At the same time, Paulina, as you will find as you grow older, life has to go on. However much we suffer today, we all have to face tomorrow."

"I know that," Paulina said, "and perhaps it would be selfish to expect every day to be happy when other people are suffering."

"That is a good philosophy but a poor consolation," Sir Christopher said drily.

Paulina kissed his cheek.

"I shall go with the Princess," she said. "But I shall

be counting the days until I come back here to you, Papa. I love being with you, I love talking to you, and most of all I love listening to the things you say in that deep voice which makes everything seem worth listening to."

"You are flattering me!" Sir Christopher replied. "But I like it."

He put his arms around her and held her closely to him. Then he said:

"Promise me, my precious, that you will be very careful with yourself. Russian men are very attractive, very eloquent both with their eyes and the words that come so smoothly to their lips. But make no mistake, they marry because it is advantageous, and for no other reason."

Paulina rubbed her cheek against his.

"What you are saying in polite words, dearest Papa, is that the Russian aristocrats of the Court will make love to me when they have no intention of making me their wife."

"That is putting it frankly, but truthfully," Sir Christopher agreed. "As with members of the Royal Family, no Russian noble can marry without permission from the Tsar, who in most cases chooses their wives to suit himself, and there is no question of challenging his decision."

"Of one thing we can be certain, and it is that His Imperial Majesty, Emperor of all the Russias, will not concern himself with Princess Margarita's Lady-in-Waiting, who has nothing to recommend her except that her father is the best-looking Diplomat in Europe."

Sir Christopher laughed.

"As far as your status is concerned, that is undoubtedly a fact!"

"Then do not worry about me! You know I always kept at arm's-length those very ardent Italian gentlemen who recited the poems of Byron and all the other poets without drawing breath."

"I think you handled them with great skill," Sir Christopher approved. "But the 'Russian Eagles,' as they are called, are known for making a woman's heart beat faster and turning their heads invariably in one direction."

"I shall always be on my guard," Paulina promised, "and will not only close my ears but lock my door!"

To her surprise, her father did not smile but his arms round her tightened.

"I must be mad to let you go," he said almost as if he was speaking to himself. "Russia is not like other countries, and the Russians have a way about them that has been the despair and ruin of many lovely women."

"Then all I can say is that they must be very foolish to be carried away to the extent that they lose both their hearts and their heads," Paulina answered.

She told herself as she spoke that it would never happen to her.

Then she could not help recalling how many women when they were in love with her father had behaved with an astonishing indiscretion.

'I suppose being in love does make one reckless,' she thought.

Then she remembered that she was English and people in England kept their emotions under control and thought before they acted.

She and her mother had often laughed at the extravagances, the over-emotionalism, and the unrestrained gesticulations of foreigners.

"They cannot help it," Lady Handley had said more than once. "We were brought up as children not to cry in public, not to lose our tempers, and that sort of self-discipline stands one in good stead all through life."

Paulina had always remembered this when she had seen women wailing unrestrainedly at the loss of somebody they loved, and men threatening to shoot themselves because they were frustrated in attaining their desires.

It all seemed to her theatrical and somehow insincere, just as the compliments she had been paid in Italy had made her want to laugh rather than to listen to them seriously.

"I will be all right," she said now, "and when I fall in love it will be with a nice, staid, sensible Englishman! We will do nothing out of the ordinary, but just get married and live happily ever afterwards."

"That is what I pray and hope will happen," Sir Christopher said, "but, my dearest child, love is unpredictable, and when you fall in love you will find that good resolutions have a habit of flying out the window."

Chapter Two

"I am frightened!" Princess Margarita said in a low voice.

Paulina turned from the port-hole where she had been looking out to sea.

"Frightened?" she queried.

She realized that the Princess was speaking to her in a secretive manner, because the language she was using was English.

Before they had left the Palace at Altauss, the Grand Duke Louis had called both the Princess and Paulina into his private room.

"I want you both to listen to me," he had said in a serious voice.

Paulina had looked at him apprehensively, wondering what he was about to say.

The Grand Duke paused for a moment as if he was feeling for words. Then he said:

"I think you are both educated enough to be aware that Russia is different from other countries and that the Secret Police have a reputation which is notorious all over Europe."

Paulina had heard this from her father, but she doubted if the Princess was aware of it.

"Since Tsar Nicholas came to the throne," the Grand Duke continued, "he has reorganized the Secret Police and formed them into a new department known as the 'Third Section.'"

"It sounds frightening, Papa," the Princess exclaimed.

"It is," the Grand Duke said quietly. "The Tsar has placed his close friend Count Benckendorff in charge and has ordered that its function is to act as 'the nation's moral Physician' in every town in Russia."

As he spoke he thought that his daughter was looking bewildered, but he guessed that Paulina as a Diplomat's daughter had some idea of the powers that had been given to the Third Section.

Paulina was in fact aware that it had become notorious for its close scrutiny of intellectuals and had also terrified ordinary people. But her father had been somewhat evasive about explaining the situation to her in more detail.

"I tell you this," the Grand Duke continued, "to ensure that you both will be very careful what you say in any Palace in Russia, in fact anywhere where you can be overheard."

"You mean that spies will be deliberately listening to us?" the Princess enquired.

"Not only will they be listening," the Grand Duke said somewhat grimly, "but anything you say will be repeated to the Tsar."

"Why should he be interested?" Princess Margarita enquired.

The Grand Duke smiled.

"Russians from the highest to the lowest are notoriously curious, and the Tsar likes to keep a very close watch on his subjects, of which, my dearest child, you will now be one."

"It seems to me ridiculous that I cannot talk to anybody without it being listened to and discussed later!" the Princess Margarita exclaimed petulantly.

"I agree with you," the Grand Duke said, "and you must make sure that in your own Palace this does not occur."

"You may be quite sure I shall do that," the Princess replied.

The girls had not discussed between themselves what the Grand Duke had said, but now Paulina was aware that Margarita was deliberately talking in a language which she thought the average Russian would not understand.

At the same time, to make it more difficult, Paulina answered her in Hungarian.

"Why are you frightened?" she asked.

As she spoke she moved nearer to Margarita and sat down on the side of the satin-covered sofa on which she was resting.

They had travelled in great luxury and comfort across Prussia, staying with the Grand Duke's relatives on the way and being feted in a manner which showed clearly that they not only approved but were delighted at the marriage the Princess was to make with the approval of the Tsar.

At Stattin the Tsar's private yacht, the *Ischora*, was waiting for them.

When they went aboard, Paulina had the feeling that they were crossing a boundary from friendly territory into one which was so different that it felt almost as if it was alien both to her and to the Princess.

However, the first night after they had steamed out to sea, Paulina was too delighted with the yacht to be concerned with anything else.

It was certainly different from any other vessel she had seen before. The cabins were decorated with panels of coloured woods and furnished with extremely valuable furniture, besides luxurious carpets and satin curtains.

To welcome them aboard there was Admiral of the Fleet Prince Grundorinski, and a younger man, Count Stroganov.

They were extremely affable and obviously ready

to flatter the Princess and show her how warm her reception would be once she reached St. Petersburg.

The food was delicious, and while they dined, musicians played Russian music softly enough not to interfere with the conversation.

They had travelled quite a long way during the day before reaching Stettin, and both the Princess and Paulina were so weary that when they retired to their own cabins they just said good-night to each other and had no private conversation.

Now after breakfast they were alone and Paulina was aware that the Princess was longing to confide in her.

"I am frightened," she said, "because when Papa leaves I shall be . . . alone, and I am not sure that I wish to . . . marry the Grand Duke . . . or . . . anybody else."

Paulina smiled before she replied:

"Of course you have to be married, and you are so beautiful that there will always be men who will wish to marry you. But as you are well aware, because the Tsar has given his approval it is socially a very brilliant marriage."

Princess Margarita did not speak for a moment, but put out her hand to hold on to Paulina as if she were a lifeline in a dangerous sea.

"Supposing," she said in a whisper, "that when I . . . see him I . . . hate him?"

It was a thought that had already crossed Paulina's mind, and as they travelled towards Stettin she had wondered what she herself would be feeling if she were going to a strange country to marry a man she had never seen or had forgotten what he looked like.

"I should be terrified!" she confessed.

She had known then that she would never, however hard anybody might try to persuade her, agree to marry a man for any reason except that she loved him.

She would not have been a Diplomat's daughter if she had not been aware that there was no question of

Royal personages being allowed to choose their own partners in life.

Now looking at Princess Margarita she realized that she was really frightened, and although they were the same age, she knew that in experience as well as in intellect she was the elder of the two.

"It will be all right," she said soothingly, "I know it will be. Although you did not notice the Grand Duke, he fell in love with you, and I am sure, since everybody says how charming he is, that when you meet you will fall in love with him."

"But suppose I do . . . not?" Princess Margarita persisted.

"You will," Paulina said positively, hoping she could almost compel the Princess into a more optimistic frame of mind.

The Princess rose to her feet and walked towards the port-hole.

She looked out at the sea, which was grey because the sky was cloudy and there was no sign of the sun.

Paulina moved towards her and when they were standing close together the Princess said almost beneath her breath:

"If I hate him . . . I shall run away!"

She drew in her breath. Then she added:

"Promise me, promise me, Paulina, that if I have to do that you will come with me."

"Of course I will, dearest," Paulina said, "but I assure you it will not be necessary! Your father has said that the Grand Duke is a man of whom he thoroughly approves, and I know he would not let you marry him otherwise."

"Papa is not thinking of me but of Altauss," the Princess said petulantly. "Oh, Paulina, you are so lucky, so very, very lucky that you are not Royal."

It was what Paulina herself was thinking, but she thought it would be a mistake to say so. Instead she said in Italian:

"I think we should be very careful what we say to each other. You would not wish the Tsar to know what you are thinking."

"That is another thing that frightens me," the Princess said. "Who is listening to us? Who is going to run tittle-tattling to His Imperial Majesty and tell him I am frightened?"

"Well, if they do, it will be understandable," Paulina said with a smile.

"Not to me," the Princess said sharply. "I want to be happy, I want to be at home and be with all those delightful young *Aides-de-Camp* who dance so well and say such pretty things to me."

Paulina laughed.

"You know you would soon grow bored with them! What they say today is exactly what they repeat tomorrow and the day after."

Princess Margarita laughed too.

"That is true, but do you think the Russians will be any more original?"

"We can only wait and find out," Paulina replied.

The next day the weather was sunny and the sea was calm, and they saw the towers of Tallinn, which the Admiral told them was exactly twenty-four hours from St. Petersburg.

That night the Northern Lights appeared and the sea was like glass. After dinner Paulina and the Princess, wrapped in furs, went on deck with the gentlemen, and the Russian crew were assembled to dance and sing.

Paulina had expected that the first time she saw Russian dancing it would be exciting, but she had not anticipated that it would have such grace when it was performed by amateurs.

Sometimes the way they leapt in the air had a grotesque savagery about it, but there was also something beguiling and their singing touched a chord in her that she had not expected.

Her father, being musical, had taken Paulina to the Opera in Italy, and some of the great singers had come to the Embassy when there were parties to entertain the guests.

But the Russian singing was different and she knew that the emotions they evoked with their strange melodies created in her both a physical and a spiritual reaction that she had not expected.

She felt her shoulders swaying, she felt her heart beating, and she felt too as if she reached out towards the stars for something she did not understand.

Only when the performance sank into silence and the Grand Duke led the applause did Paulina feel as if she had passed through a strange emotional experience and had suddenly descended from the skies back to earth.

When they went down to their cabins that night she was surprised when the Princess said:

"I certainly hope the entertainment in St. Petersburg will be better than that!"

"Better?" Paulina queried.

"Did you not see how rough and dirty many of the crew were? And as a musical effort I should have thought they might have provided us with something more sophisticated."

Paulina did not reply. She merely kissed the Princess good-night and went to her own cabin.

When she was alone she knew that she had found something Russian that had appealed to her while it had left the Princess untouched.

*   *   *

The following morning they saw Kronstadt, where in the enormous granite harbour there was a long line of battle-ships while the sea was littered with vessels.

There were Men-o'-War, cargo-ships, frigates, steam-boats, packets, floating light-houses—vessels of all shapes and sizes and from all countries.

Soon they were in the Neva and ahead of them was St. Petersburg.

To Paulina it was exactly as she had expected and even more lovely than her father's description of it had suggested.

The great blue and green domes topped with gold and the gilded spires gave it the impression of a fairy-city and she only hoped that it looked as romantic to the Princess as it did to her.

There seemed to be an enormous number of gorgeously arrayed Courtiers waiting for them as the yacht drew alongside the quay, and, as they had been warned, the Grand Duke Vladirvitch was the first to come aboard.

This was the moment, Paulina knew, that the Princess had been dreading.

She was looking very lovely, wearing one of her best gowns and a bonnet trimmed with roses, and as she curtseyed to her future husband Paulina thought that nobody could be more attractive or more alluring.

She knew as she watched that she too had been a little apprehensive as to what the Grand Duke would be like.

She had heard so many stories over the years of Princes who had been led to believe by the portraits which had been sent to them that their Royal brides were beauties, only to find that they were small, dumpy, and with bad teeth and ugly features.

The same fate often awaited a Princess who was sent across Europe to find that her bridegroom was a surly, middle-aged man, marrying for the second time only because he required an heir and having many other interests besides the woman who was to be his wife.

But the Grand Duke Vladirvitch was certainly extremely imposing.

He made an eloquent speech of welcome, kissed the Princess's hand, and looked at her in a manner which portrayed quite obviously that he would have liked to be more intimate than he was able to be at the moment.

Paulina thought it would be impossible for Margarita not to find him attractive in a white tunic decorated with gold braid, top-boots up to the knees, and a gold-plated cuirass and helmet.

The golden eagle on the crest of the helmet told her that the Grand Duke was wearing the romantic uniform of the Hussars.

"I have been counting the hours until this day," he said, still holding the Princess's hand in his. "Now you that are here, I can hardly believe that I am not still dreaming."

His voice was low and deep, and as Paulina saw a faint flush creep up Princess Margarita's cheeks she felt it would be impossible for any woman not to respond to such charming ardour.

In fact, by the time they were in the open carriage and Paulina with her back to the horses was facing the Grand Duke and the Princess, she was aware that her friend was talking excitedly and animatedly to her future husband.

But it was difficult for Paulina to think of anything at the moment except that she was seeing St. Petersburg.

Her father had warned her that everything was on a grand scale and that the immense Palaces, the enormous Squares, and the wide streets made the people look like pygmies, while the carriages shrank to the size of nut-shells.

What she had forgotten of the other things he had told her was that the great houses, which were almost as vast and magnificent as the Royal Palaces, were all painted in the family colours.

One was in white and crimson, another in rich blue, others in lilac, salmon, or yellow.

The Winter Palace, painted a heavy maroon, was

so enormous that it was hard for Paulina to realise that
it was in fact a human habitation.

There seemed to be thousands of people outside,
but she was to learn later that it was just an ordinary
crowd of coachmen, lackeys, serfs, and callers who went
in and out of the Palace every day and who appeared
always to have some special business there.

There were six carriages to carry them from the
yacht to the Palace, and their procession travelled along
the bank of the Neva. Paulina noticed that the people
moving about the streets did not seem interested nor
did they make any effort to wave to the occupants of the
carriages.

In Altauss, wherever the Grand Duke went, there
were cheers, cries of welcome, and the children would
throw flowers into his carriage, while his popularity was
obvious from the smiles on his subjects' faces.

The Russians they passed now on the roadway
either stared straight ahead of them or down on the
ground as if they were afraid to be noticed.

'They do not seem to be a very happy people,'
Paulina thought to herself, but she knew it was something she must not say to the Princess.

Inside the Palace, the liveries of the servants were
as splendid as the uniforms of the soldiers on guard,
and the Palace itself made Paulina gasp, even though
her father had warned her that it was magnificent and
positively breathtaking.

The high gold or jasper pillars, the crystal chandeliers, the pictures, and the domed ceilings in the passages were all so awe-inspiring that she found it impossible to listen to the officer escorting them, but could
only stare about her in bewilderment.

Finally they reached the Tsar's apartments, where
His Imperial Majesty and the Tsarina were waiting for
them.

"Tsar Nicholas is undoubtedly the most intimidat-

ing Sovereign in Europe," Sir Christopher had said to
Paulina before she left Altauss.

"Somebody said, I have forgotten who it was,"
Paulina replied, "that he is very handsome."

Sir Christopher laughed.

"When the Tsar visited Windsor Castle ten years
ago," he said, "the Queen said that the secret of his
awesome appearance was that his left eye was slightly
asymmetrical, like 'a nail at white heat.'"

Paulina laughed.

"What did Her Majesty mean by that?"

"She wrote," Sir Christopher replied, "*He is certainly a very striking man, and still very handsome. His
profile is beautiful, but the expression in his eyes is
formidable, and unlike anything I ever saw before.*"

As the Tsar greeted first the Grand Duke, then the
Princess, Paulina watching them understood exactly
what the Queen had meant.

The Tsar was not only formidable, but there was
something about him that was ruthless and merciless,
and she had the feeling that he was almost inhuman.

She was in fact so bemused by him that when she
was presented to the Tsarina she almost forgot to
curtsey.

Then she knew that the bird-like Prussian wife of
His Imperial Majesty was very different from her awe-
inspiring husband.

The Tsarina smiled at Paulina but did not speak,
and passed on to the other members of the entourage
that the Grand Duke Louis had brought with him from
Altauss.

Only when Paulina had followed the Princess up
the long wide staircase to the rooms that had been
allotted to them did she feel that she could breathe
naturally.

The rooms they had been given were sumptuous.
Even her own was far larger than any bedroom she had

had at Altauss or in any other diplomatic building in
which she had lived with her father.

A lady's-maid removed the Princess's travelling-
cape and bonnet, and a few seconds later Margarita
came into Paulina's room to say in English:

"What do you think of Russia, and more especially,
what do you think of the Grand Duke?"

"I think you are very lucky," Paulina answered.
"He is charming, and certainly impressive in his uniform."

"That is what I thought," the Princess said, "and
perhaps we will be happy, but I think he will also be
very dictatorial."

It was what Paulina thought too, but she was too
diplomatic to say so.

"I expect you will get used to it," she said.

The Princess came nearer to her and in a voice that
was only a whisper she said:

"The Tsar is a monster, I am sure of it! When he
touched my hand, his was cold as if it were made of
steel!"

Paulina thought the Princess was exaggerating, but
she could understand what she was feeling.

"I expect you will get used to him too," she
answered.

The Princess looked out the window.

"Where do you think they hide while they are
listening to us?" she asked.

"Inside the walls," Paulina replied.

Princess Margarita ran to one of the panelled walls,
and when she knocked on it, it sounded hollow.

Then she went to the other side of the room and
knocked again.

Paulina shook her head and the Princess came back
to her side.

"I think it is a mistake," Paulina said in a low voice,
"to let them know you suspect they are listening. If we
keep changing our language it will be difficult enough

for them to follow us. I doubt if there are enough agents available who are fluent in all the languages we know."

The Princess Margarita smiled.

"If it puzzles them, all the better!" she said. "I hate eavesdroppers!"

"So do I!" Paulina agreed. "But that is another thing we have to get used to."

That evening as they dined they learnt of the strange customs that were observed in the Palace.

For the Court and nobility the round of supper-parties and Balls began at midnight and lasted until the small hours.

The usual time to call and visit a friend was eleven o'clock in the evening. Dinner was served at about six o'clock, after which, to Paulina's and the Princess's amusement, they learnt that the ladies usually retired to bed to "rest their complexions" before reappearing at midnight, radiant and glittering with jewellery.

"Supper is never served before two o'clock in the morning," a Courtier informed them.

"Then at what time do you go to bed?" Paulina enquired.

He shrugged his shoulders.

"Seldom before four o'clock."

Paulina laughed.

"But surely that way your nights become days and your days nights?"

"It does seem like that," he agreed, "and many of us have to learn to burn the candle at both ends."

She looked at him for an explanation and he said:

"The Tsar begins work at five o'clock in the morning, and however late we have been dancing or dining, we are expected to be on duty."

"It sounds exhausting!" Paulina laughed.

The Courtier shrugged his shoulders.

"We get used to it," he said, "as you will, too."

Their first night was fairly quiet, and after they had dined at six with the Tsar and Tsarina, they had supper with some elderly relatives of the future bridegroom, who fortunately did not wish to stay up late.

"I think it is a ridiculous idea!" the Princess said when finally they reached their own bedrooms, yawning because it was long after their usual bedtime.

"You will be able to run things more normally when you have a Palace of your own," Paulina suggested.

"I shall insist upon it," the Princess replied.

At the same time, she did not sound very sure of being able to get her own way. However, Paulina thought now that at least she had accepted without further protestation the idea of marrying the Grand Duke.

There was no doubt that he was charming, and Paulina was sure that when his eyes rested on the Princess's beautiful face there was not only an expression of admiration in them but something else as well.

"I am sure he is in love with her," Paulina told herself, "and they will be very happy together."

She sent up a little prayer that this might happen.

When she slipped into her luxurious bed with its silk hangings and with the Imperial Crown embroidered on the sheets, she thought that Princess Margarita's future would be a happy one, despite the fact that Russia itself was so unpredictable.

*   *   *

Because she was tired, Paulina slept well and awoke the next morning to look out the window on the Neva, which was as golden as the domes and spires on either side of it.

"It is a beautiful city," she told herself.

At the same time, she thought that something was lacking, and she knew, although she hesitated to put it into words, that what it was that was missing was—heart.

In every other city she had visited—Rome, London, Paris, and Wildenstadt, the Capital of Altauss—she had always been conscious, besides the houses, the Churches,

and the elaborate Civic buildings, of the people themselves.

People who would laugh, who were born, married,
and died, who belonged to their country of origin and,
because they belonged, loved it.

Although she had seen very little of Russia, she
had the feeling that the great buildings erected by
Peter the Great and his successors, the towering spires
of the Churches, and the glittering domes, were all
completely separate from those who, small and insignificant, moved like ants beneath them.

It seemed to her that it was like living on two
levels, a higher and a lower, and they had no real
communication with each other.

Then as the sunshine dazzled her eyes and everything outside the Palace looked lovely, she told herself
she was being imaginative.

'I shall find out that I was wrong!' she thought.

Yet there was a strong conviction within herself
that she was right.

She stood for a long time at the window, until she
heard movements next door and knew that the Princess
too was awake.

Wearing a blue robe over her nightgown and with
her hair flowing over her shoulders, Paulina went to
her.

Princess Margarita was looking very lovely, her
eyes a little hazy with sleep and her dark hair hanging
below her waist seeming to glow with blue lights which
were echoed by the shine in her eyes.

"Good-morning, Paulina," she said. "Come and
talk to me. There are so many things I want to ask you,
but I expect we shall have to wait until we are outside
and can talk without being overheard."

"I am sure if we talk in English no-one will understand what we say," Paulina said. "I learnt last night
that very few people speak English in the Palace."

"They do not speak Russian either, which I find

extraordinary," the Princess said. "But as the Tsarina is German they speak that language as a compliment to her, although everyone prefers to converse in French."

"I agree it is all very strange," Paulina said, "but understandable."

As she spoke she knew that the Princess was not listening to her. Then she said a little shyly:

"What do you really think of Alexander?"

"I think the Grand Duke is charming!" Paulina replied.

"He said some very delightful things to me," the Princess said. "He paid me some of the nicest compliments I have ever received in my life! But... Paulina... I heard something last night that... worries me."

"What was that?" Paulina asked.

The Princess hesitated a moment before she answered:

"There have been... many women in the Grand Duke's life... and one in particular."

Paulina did not answer for a moment. She knew that it was very important that she should reassure the Princess, and what she had just said did not surprise her.

She had already learnt from her father that Russians were always passionately in love with beautiful women, and it was as much a part of their lives as their horses, their search for amusement, and their allegiance to the Regiment in which they served.

After a moment she said a little hesitatingly:

"The Grand Duke is... attractive... so it is to be expected that there are... ladies to tell him so."

"I can understand that," the Princess said, "but when last night one of the relatives of the Tsar to whom I was speaking said how much he will give up when he marries, I knew he was speaking of the... women who obviously have... played a... large part in his... life."

"He is young and it is to be expected that he should be a man."

"I thought as we were coming here," the Princess said in a low voice, "that he was waiting . . . alone for my arrival."

Paulina had thought very much the same thing, but when she was in Italy with her father she had realised that the young Aristocrats always spent their time with beautiful women to whom they made love whether they were married or unmarried or, like the Grand Duke, betrothed.

Because she knew she must console her friend, she said after a moment:

"Most men like the company of women, but that is not to say that they love them. If the Grand Duke loves you, which I think he does, then that is something altogether very different."

"How can I be sure . . . how can I be sure?" the Princess asked. "And supposing, Paulina, after he has married me he still wants other women?"

Paulina suddenly felt as if she too was bewildered and even puzzled.

She wished her mother were there to help the Princess, and she knew that if she were in the same position she would feel not jealous but apprehensive of the women who filled a man's life.

Because she did not speak, the Princess went on:

"How can I be sure that he is not marrying me simply because he wants to have a wife and children? How can I know that as soon as we are married he will not go back to the women who amused him before, and leave me alone?"

She gave a little cry of horror.

"In Russia I shall be . . . very . . . very alone."

"You will have your brother," Paulina said quickly.

The Princess looked at her in surprise.

"So I shall," she said almost beneath her breath. "I had forgotten Maximus. The Tsar told me last night that he has been in Moscow and will return to St. Petersburg tomorrow."

"Then you must talk to him about the Grand Duke," Paulina said. "He will reassure you and will also be able to tell you more about him."

"I want to believe what he says to me," the Princess said. "I want to believe that he is speaking the truth . . . at the same time . . ."

Paulina sat down beside the bed and took Princess Margarita's hand in hers.

"Listen," she said. "What you have said to me you must say quite frankly and openly to the Grand Duke himself. Tell him how you feel, tell him what the ladies to whom you were speaking last night told you. I suspect that they were being jealous and spiteful, but if it worries you, it is his right to console you."

The Princess held Paulina's hand tightly in hers.

"Do you really think I can . . . talk to him like . . . that?"

"Why not?" Paulina asked. "Surely it is better to be frank and honest with each other from the very beginning of your relationship, and I think he will understand."

"Why should you think that?" the Princess asked.

"Because I have travelled with Papa," Paulina answered, "and as I have been to many different countries, I like to believe that I can trust my instinct about people."

She smiled before she added:

"I am aware what they are like not only on the surface but in their hearts and souls, and I think that underneath his very impressive appearance your Grand Duke is a man you can trust."

The Princess gave a little cry.

"Oh, Paulina, I hope you are right! I hope I can trust him, and I think, I really think, that I am beginning to fall in love with him!"

"That is what I hoped you would do," Paulina said. "But you have to remember that he has had a long life before he met and loved you, and of course there have

been other women in it, women who have meant a lot
to him, as he has meant a lot to them."

The Princess's hand tightened on hers.

"I expect if I talk to him as I have been talking to
you, he will think I am childish and rather stupid."

"Why should he think that?" Paulina enquired.

"Because I am so ignorant about men like him. As
you know, he is different from all those I have met at
home."

Paulina thought this was true.

The young men with whom they had danced at the
Palace had all been young, she thought, and somewhat
unsophisticated compared to the Italians.

Aloud she said:

"I think Russians are very sensitive in their characters, and, perhaps because they are Slavs, they feel
things more deeply than European men do. It makes
them difficult for us to understand. At the same time, I
am certain that if the Grand Duke loves you and you
love him, it will be something very wonderful that you
have never known before."

"That is what I want," the Princess said. "Oh,
Paulina, I want it so much. If I love him and then lose
him, then it will be worse for me than anything I have
ever experienced."

Paulina was surprised. She had not expected the
Princess to be so perceptive.

Now she was aware that this was the beginning of
falling in love; the uncertainty, the need to be reassured,
the yearning which in fact could only be assuaged by
one person: the man with whom Margarita was falling
in love.

Because she felt it important, Paulina said:

"Talk to the Grand Duke. Talk to him intimately
about yourself, and try to understand him. Perhaps he
is feeling much as you are, unsure and a little frightened of you. After all, if you find him strange and

difficult to understand, he could be feeling exactly the same way about you."

"I never thought of that," the Princess said simply, "but I will try, Paulina. I will try . . . I really will!"

"I am sure your brother will help you," Paulina said, "and what is more, you have a long time in which to get to know each other before you are married."

The Princess looked at her in surprise.

"Did you not hear what the Tsar said last night?"

"What did he say?" Paulina asked.

"He told Papa there was no point in waiting, and he has decided that our marriage shall take place in a week's time."

"A week?" Paulina cried. "But that seems extraordinary!"

"Papa thought the same, but the Tsar has made up his mind, and there will be no chance of his changing it."

Paulina went from the bed to walk across to the window.

She thought it was typical of the high-handed, autocratic way in which the Tsar behaved.

Surely he must realise that it was difficult enough for the Princess to come to Russia, and to be engaged to a man she met only once before, without putting the wedding forward in such a precipitate manner.

She had become aware as soon as she arrived in the Palace that what she had heard before had not been exaggerated.

The Tsar was a law unto himself, and to everybody else he was the law.

He gave orders that must be obeyed, and if they were not, then the consequences were too terrible even to contemplate.

Like a gust of sudden wind the Princess Margarita was to be married off in a week to a strange man in a strange country, where her allegiance would be to a

strange Monarch who was deciding their lives, without
their even having the chance of being consulted.

'It is wrong,' Paulina thought but she knew there
would be no point in saying so.

At the same time, she felt herself shiver.

Everything was too big, too enormous. It was like
the Palace itself, so vast that she felt she would never
find her way round it.

She looked out at the Neva and thought that too
was the biggest river she had ever seen.

She had the feeling that Margarita, like all the
other people in Russia, was being carried along on its
waters, and there was no escape from the force which
compelled them relentlessly to move towards their fate.

Chapter Three

"I find your daughter as delightful as your son," the Tsar said.

"That is extremely gracious of Your Imperial Majesty," the Grand Duke replied formally.

The Tsar put his hand on his shoulder.

"We are old friends, my dear Louis, and I can tell you that I am glad I can forge a clear link between our two countries. I shall promote Alexander, and I do not think you will be disappointed in what I have in store for your son, Maximus."

"It is difficult for me to express my gratitude," the Grand Duke murmured.

The two men walked as if by instinct towards the window.

Outside, the sun was shining and everything seemed to glitter.

"In a few days we will go to the country, to Tsarskoe-Selo," the Tsar said, "and I shall be glad to get out of the city."

"You will not wait until after the wedding?" the Grand Duke enquired.

The Tsar shook his head.

"It will be easy to drive in from the country, and it will give those who are gathering by the roadside a chance to see the bride."

He smiled before he said:

"I have made my plans, and I do not think you will find anything amiss."

"I am sure that would be impossible." the Grand Duke murmured, knowing that if there was anything of which he did not approve, he would not be able to say so.

He too thought that the Tsar was being rather high-handed in marrying Margarita off so quickly, and he had an uncomfortable feeling, which he dared not express aloud, that there was some hidden reason for it.

But the Tsar was talking of Maximus.

"Your son has done brilliantly, absolutely brilliantly in our battles with Shamyl," he said. "One of his rewards will, I know, please you. The other is slightly more subtle."

The Tsar gave an unexpected chuckle as he added:

"I expect you have already learnt that he is very enamoured of the Princess Natasha."

"I have heard of it," the Grand Duke replied.

"She is very alluring," the Tsar said, "and her husband at this moment is on a special mission in Georgia."

The Grand Duke was aware of the innuendo in the Tsar's words and murmured again:

"I can only thank you."

The Tsar laughed.

"I think your son will do that."

There was an interruption as another guest came into the room and there was no chance of further conversation on the subject.

*   *   *

Changing for dinner in the bedroom to which he had hurried on his arrival, His Royal Highness Prince Maximus of Altauss glanced ruefully at the clock on the mantelpiece.

He was aware that he would have arrived earlier if he had not lingered over luncheon with a very attractive hostess on whom he had called on his way to St. Petersburg.

It had been impossible for him to leave as soon as the meal was finished, for she drew him into her private Sitting-Room and it was quite obvious from the expression in her eyes and the smile on her lips that what she had to say to him was both private and intimate.

Much later, when he tried to say good-bye, she had clung to him, saying, as many women had said to him before:

"When shall I see you again, Maximus? You know how much I hate to lose you, and we are so seldom alone together."

"If it is possible, I will call when I rejoin the Regiment," the Prince promised.

He kissed her hand and looked into her eyes in a manner that was particularly his own, and which invariably made a woman's heart beat more quickly.

"Thank you, Zenia," he said softly, "you are very lovely and very generous to me."

"How can I be anything else?" Zenia asked, and there was an unmistakable little sob in her voice.

She had loved him for a long time, and although they had had a quick, fiery, *affaire de coeur*, it had, when the Prince left for the Caucasus, faded into an uneasy friendship.

Zenia was well aware that wherever the Prince was there would always be women, and it was inevitable that she would be supplanted in his affections.

She was too experienced not to realise that she was one of many, and even in the depths of the country where her husband had great responsibilities she had heard rumors of Prince Maximus's infatuation for the Princess Natasha, and had hated her.

It was of Natasha that the Prince was thinking as he rode on towards the Winter Palace.

He had met her three months ago and found her

more alluring than anyone he had seen for a very long time.

The way her Slavic eyes slanted upwards at the corners, the twist of her red lips, the perfect oval of her face, and the purple darkness of her hair intrigued him.

Without really being conscious of it, he had been counting the days until he saw her again.

She had written to him passionate letters which seemed to the Prince somewhat indiscreet, and although he had little time to reply, he had let her know when on the Tsar's orders he would be coming to St. Petersburg to greet his sister.

He was quite certain that Natasha would somehow contrive to meet him there.

She was a favourite with both the Tsar and the Tsarina, and the Prince suspected that the former had other uses for her besides that of entertaining one of his favourite Major-Generals.

He had been too long at Court not to know that the Tsar made diplomatic use of attractive women to extract political secrets from the representatives of other countries more effectively than any man could do.

When he had first met Natasha she had been constantly at the side of an attractive English Diplomat who had been sent, the Tsar was convinced, to find out for the Foreign Office in London the Russian intentions in respect to various European matters.

She must in fact have finished her assignment when they met, for two nights later she had come to his room through a secret entrance, and had made it quite clear that she asked nothing from him except the touch of his lips and the burning fire that their need of each other engendered.

"You are very beautiful, Natasha!" the Prince had said to her as dawn was breaking in the sky outside.

"I want you to think so," she had answered in a seductive voice.

She had pulled his head to hers, and there was no

need for them to talk, for the fire that had flamed in the
night blazed up again and consumed them both.

It was impossible for the Prince not to think of
Natasha when he was fighting in the wild, towering
mountains of the Caucasus, and in some strange way
the perpendicular rock cliffs, topped by eagles'-nest
aôuls which hung over ravines so deep that no light
ever penetrated the abyss where torrents raged, reminded
him of Natasha.

They had the same mystery, the same unpredict-
ability, and perhaps they gave him the same desire to
be the victor and master that he was with her.

Prince Maximus was not usually introspective about
his love-affairs.

Because he was so handsome, attractive, and had
an irrepressible vitality, there were always lovely wom-
en trying to attract his attention and drawing him by
what he told himself was an irresistible force.

As his valet gave the last touch to his tunic, the
Prince did not wait to look at himself in the mirror.

Instead, knowing that he had only a few minutes to
spare before he reached the Tsar's apartments, he ran
from his bedroom down the long corridor which led to
the wide staircase.

Still hurrying, he went towards the Royal Apartments, passing Chevaliers Gardes, lackeys, Courtiers,
and Court messengers, with whom the Palace passages
abounded, but none of them took any notice of him,
knowing too well that no-one had enough time to get
from here to there.

The Prince was breathless by the time he reached
a guarded double door behind which the Tsar and his
family lived when they were in residence.

There was only a short pause while sentries opened
the door so that the resplendent Major-Domo could
come forward to announce him.

The Prince had no need to give his name—he was
too well known to the Royal Family—and pompously,

very conscious of his own importance, the Major-Domo in his colourful livery walked ahead of him.

The Prince raised a hand to smooth his hair into place and also checked to make sure that his uniform was correct and tidy.

Officers had been sent to Siberia for having a button undone or a medal out of place, and however well one might know the Tsar and imagine that one was in favour, his moods were so unpredictable that they could change as quickly as a heart-beat.

"I cannot permit that even one person should dare to defy my wishes the moment he has been made exactly aware of them," the Tsar had written in the margin of a report soon after he came to the throne.

His wishes had grown more complicated as the years had passed, while his determination to be obeyed had become obsessive.

But tonight, at least, the Tsar was in a good humour.

The moment the Prince was announced there was a smile on his usually severe face, and he even walked two paces forward to greet him.

"My dear Maximus!" he exclaimed as the Prince approached him. "I am delighted to see you, and I have been telling your father of your exploits in the Caucasus, of which we are exceedingly proud."

The Prince bowed his acknowledgements, then he was at his father's side, clasping his hand.

"It is good to see you, Papa!" he exclaimed.

He knew as he spoke that he had missed his father, even though life in Russia was exciting and adventurous and everything he enjoyed.

"It is good to see you too, my boy," the Grand Duke replied.

"Is Margarita here?" the Prince asked.

He glanced round as he spoke, aware to his surprise that although it was nearly time for dinner there was nobody else present.

"She is here," the Grand Duke replied, "and is to be married in a week!"

"A week?" Prince Maximus asked in astonishment.

He tried to expostulate that this was surely too hasty, but the Tsar said coldly:

"On my instructions. I think it best that it should take place immediately, and there would be no point in your father returning to Altauss to come back again in two months, as he had planned at first."

"No, of course not, Sire," the Prince agreed.

At the same time he looked at his father questioningly, wondering what was the reason for such haste and if it had his approval.

However, there was no time to say any more.

The Tsar walked ahead to the Salon next door, where the other members of the party were waiting.

The Prince went first to kiss the Tsarina's hand. Then Princess Margarita with a little cry was at his side, raising her face to his.

"Maximus! Maximus! It is so wonderful to see you!" she exclaimed. "We have missed you at home more than I can ever say."

The Prince kissed his sister on the cheek.

"I have missed you too," he said, "and I can see you are far prettier than when I went away."

"That is what I hoped you would think," she answered.

The Prince laughed and kissed her again, then realised who was standing behind her.

He held out his hand to the Grand Duke Vladirvitch, who said:

"I only hope that in the future Margarita will greet me as enthusiastically as she has greeted you."

"I know that is what we both hope," the Prince said with a smile, "and let me congratulate you on your engagement."

"I am very much to be congratulated," the Grand

Duke Alexander said, "and I hope you will give the marriage your approval."

"But of course," the Prince replied lightly. "I feel sure that you will make my sister very happy."

"That is what I intend to do," the Grand Duke said.

The Prince felt his sister's hand on his arm.

"I want to introduce you," Margarita said, "to the friend who has come with me from Altauss as my Lady-in-Waiting."

She turned him round and said:

"Paulina, this is my brother, Maximus, of whom we have so often talked. I hope you two will be friends."

Paulina curtseyed as the Prince bowed.

She had been watching him ever since he came into the room, and she thought he was even better-looking than the portraits of him which she had seen at the Palace at Altauss.

He was also taller than most of the Russians in the room and had a lithe, athletic grace which she appreciated came from hard riding and taking a great deal of exercise.

As she rose and raised her eyes to the Prince, he held out his hand.

"*Enchanté, Mademoiselle.*"

"No, no!" the Princess cried. "You must speak English to her. Paulina is English! The daughter of Sir Christopher Handley, who has come to Altauss as the British Minister."

At this Maximus smiled.

"English!" he said. "I was certainly not expecting you to have an English Lady-in-Waiting, Margarita. What has happened to Baroness Schwaez?"

"I told Papa that if I had to bring that boring old woman with me to Russia I would refuse to go!"

The Prince laughed.

"I can see that Miss Handley does not fit into that category."

Now he was speaking in English, and Paulina was aware that like his sister he was not only very fluent but had only a trace of an accent.

"It is a great privilege to be here with Her Royal Highness," she said, as she felt she should say something.

She did not know why, but she felt somewhat shy in addressing the Prince.

Because she had travelled so much with her father ever since her childhood, Paulina was seldom shy, but there was something about the Prince that made her feel it was difficult to meet his eyes, and unaccountably she found it hard to speak directly to him.

This was such an unusual experience and so unlike herself that she thought she must appear very foolish, and it was with a conscious effort that she forced herself to look up into his eyes as she waited for his reply.

She thought, although she might have been mistaken, that he was looking at her in a somewhat strange way.

Then the Princess commanded his attention and a moment later the Tsar introduced him to the other ladies who were present.

There was no move yet towards the Dining-Room and Paulina realised that surprisingly it was long past the usual hour at which the Tsar, who was meticulously punctual, insisted on having dinner.

Then the door of the Salon opened and the Major-Domo announced:

"The Princess Natasha Bragadtov, Your Imperial Majesty."

Every head turned and Paulina watching the newcomer thought she was the most outstanding person she had yet seen in the Winter Palace.

She wore a gown that glittered with every movement she made, her swan-like neck was encircled with a necklace of huge emeralds, the same stones hung glittering from her ears, and the tiara on her dark head was also of emeralds

But it was not only her clothes and her jewellery that were so striking. The slanting eyes and the manner in which she moved had a feline grace that made Paulina think of a wild animal.

"She is like a tigress," she told herself as the Princess hurried forward to sweep down in a deep curtsey before the Tsar.

"Forgive me—forgive me," she said in a husky voice that seemed somehow in keeping with her appearance. "I know I am late, I know I deserve to be sent in chains to the deepest dungeon! The only excuse I have to offer is that I was attempting to look beautiful for you—My Imperial Majesty!"

She was so dramatic that the Tsar laughed.

"For me, Natasha?" he enquired. "That I very much doubt! But dinner is waiting and you can make the rest of your apologies later."

As he spoke he turned to offer his arm to the Tsarina, and as they moved ahead Paulina noticed that the Princess Natasha's hand went out towards Prince Maximus, who bent over it in a manner which told her without words that they were very close friends.

They were placed beside each other at dinner, and because Paulina was between two rather boring dinner-partners who concentrated more on their food than on conversation with her, she was able to watch the Prince.

She had learnt, as she had told the Princess Margarita, to see at times beneath the surface of the face that a person presented to the world.

She was aware now that the Princess Natasha was talking to Prince Maximus in a way that was not only very intimate but also very enticing.

With every flutter of her long, dark eye-lashes and every twist of her red mouth she appeared provocative and at the same time inviting.

As they talked, her long fingers touched the Prince's

arm or his hand in a manner which Paulina thought proclaimed their intimacy.

She noticed that the Princess Margarita was deeply engrossed in conversation with the Grand Duke Alexander, the Tsar was talking across the table to the Grand Duke Louis, and the Tsarina seemed more interested in her son, who sat at one side of her, than in anybody else.

The rest of the party was made up of Court officials who Paulina thought on the whole were exceedingly good-looking, besides being very fashionably dressed.

She had learnt that all Russian Aristocrats bought their clothes from Paris, and she felt that her own pretty but not very expensive gown was easily outshone by every other woman present.

Then she told herself that as a mere Lady-in-Waiting she should be subservient and certainly should not push herself forward.

At the same time, she hoped that Prince Maximus would not think she looked a too insignificant and unattractive companion for his sister.

Because she was thinking of him she must have been looking at him directly, for unexpectedly he looked across the table at her and their eyes met.

It was, Paulina thought, almost as if they vibrated to each other in a way that was a physical impact.

For what seemed a long time, although it might only have been the passing of a second, her eyes were held captive before she was able to look away from him.

The dinner did not take long, for the Tsar was not a great eater, and when it was over the Tsarina dismissed her guests, saying they must all rest because they were to return at eleven o'clock for what was to be a small Ball in honour of the Princess Margarita and her brother, Prince Maximus.

This was something they had not expected, and as they went upstairs to their bedrooms Margarita exclaimed:

"Can you imagine anything more ridiculous than having dressed once to have to undress and start again?"

"It does seem a waste of time," Paulina agreed, "but as the Ball is in your honour, you will have to wear something very elaborate and very striking."

"I cannot think why we were not told the plans earlier," the Princess grumbled. "This is one of my best gowns, although naturally I have a great number of others."

As she had brought her trousseau with her, Paulina knew this was true.

She herself was in a far worse position than the Princess, since having only a few really grand gowns she did not know which she should change into for the second part of the evening.

They had just reached their bedrooms when they heard footsteps behind them.

Paulina turned round first and saw that Prince Maximus was following them.

He looked very attractive as he came hurrying up the stairs.

The decorations on his tunic glittered in the light of the chandeliers and she thought too that his eyes shone as if he was excited.

The Princess gave a little cry of excitement.

"Maximus! Have you come to talk to me?"

"Of course I have!" he said. "At least we can have a little time together before we have to change for the Ball."

"I was just saying to Paulina how ridiculous it is to have to dress and undress twice every evening," Margarita answered.

"They certainly do things bigger, if not better, in Russia," the Prince said with a laugh.

By now they had reached the top of the staircase, and as the Princess walked into the *Boudoir* that was on one side of her bedroom, Paulina would have gone to her own room.

"No, no, Paulina, come and talk to us. I want you to get to know Maximus," the Princess said.

Paulina hesitated, looking at the Prince as if for confirmation.

"That is something I am very anxious to do," he said quietly.

Paulina wanted to smile at him politely to show that she appreciated the compliment, but somehow once again it was difficult and she found herself turning her head away shyly as she followed the Princess into her *Boudoir.*

It was a pretty room with panelled walls painted blue and rose-coloured damask curtains embroidered with a gold fringe.

The Princess sat down on a sofa and said:

"If you want to talk to us intimately, you had better speak a language which those who may be listening will find hard to follow."

She spoke in Hungarian, then added in Spanish:

"Paulina and I reckon that the listening-posts hidden between the walls will have to be packed to suffocation if they are anxious to understand everything we say!"

The Prince threw back his head and laughed.

"Whose idea was this?" he enquired.

"I think it was Paulina's," the Princess replied. "Fortunately we have been practising our languages with each other, and we know about six different ones between us."

"I had no idea you were so erudite," Prince Maximus said, "and I am full of admiration for your ingenuity!"

He was speaking to his sister but he was looking at Paulina, and in a very different tone of voice Margarita said:

"Paulina has advised me to ask you about Alexander. Since I have been in St. Petersburg I have already heard . . . things which . . . worry me."

"What sort of things?" the Prince asked sharply.

"That although he says he has set his heart on our marriage, it may not be . . . true," the Princess answered frankly.

Paulina felt this was a rather embarrassing conversation to have in her presence.

But, knowing Margarita as well as she did, she knew that she was relying on her to press her brother to tell her the things she wanted to know, and she was afraid that if they were alone he would somehow evade telling her the truth or perhaps refuse to answer any of her questions.

She saw that what the Princess had said had taken the Prince by surprise.

Sitting down in a comfortable armchair, he looked at his sister in a manner which told Paulina that he was turning over in his mind what he would reply, until finally he said:

"The Grand Duke has been on his own for a long time. He must be thirty-five years old, and you cannot expect him to have lived like a monk for all those years."

"No, of course not," Princess Margarita said, "but why do we have to be married so quickly before we really have a chance to get to know each other?"

"I am sure that is entirely the Tsar's doing," Prince Maximus replied. "The Grand Duke, whom I have always liked and admired, would have been sensible enough to want to get to know you well before he made you his wife."

"Then why can he not persuade the Tsar to postpone it?" Margarita asked.

"No-one could possibly persuade the Tsar to do anything he does not wish to do," the Prince replied. "He has always been extremely kind to me, but quite frankly, Margarita, I would hate to cross him in any way. I am sure you are well aware of his reputation, as I am."

The Prince spoke in a low voice and Paulina noticed

that he was now speaking in Hungarian, but not quite so fluently and accurately as his sister spoke the language.

"You have not answered my question," the Princess said.

"I think it would be a mistake for me to do so," the Prince replied. "I want you to be happy, Margarita, and I cannot imagine that any man would wish for the ghosts of his past to go with him on his honeymoon."

Paulina thought that would certainly apply where he was concerned, and involuntarily a faint smile came to her lips.

As if the Prince read her thoughts, he said:

"Yes, Miss Handley, I am speaking personally at this moment."

Paulina looked at him in a startled manner.

She had not expected him to be so perceptive that he would know what she was thinking, and as if she felt he rebuked her, she lowered her eyes and said quietly:

"I am . . . sorry."

"Perhaps it is I who should apologise."

"There is no need," Paulina said. "But I shall have to try to have no secrets that I do not wish revealed."

"I think it would be very difficult for you to have secrets or to be in the least deceptive," the Prince said.

They were talking to each other as if there were nobody else in the room, and after a moment Princess Margarita said in an aggrieved tone:

"I do not understand what you are talking about."

"Forgive us," the Prince said. "But I am in fact, Margarita, thinking of you."

"In what way?" the Princess asked almost defiantly. "I am thinking of my happiness."

"And so am I, as it happens," her brother replied, "and I know your happiness will be in looking forward, no back, where your husband is concerned. In other words, every man has a 'Bluebeard cupboard' and has no wish for it to be opened by his wife."

The Princess made a little sound of exasperation before she said:

"You are being infuriating, Maximus, as you always are! You are prepared to leave me alone in this huge country with a man I hardly know, and if I am unhappy with him what am I do do?"

"You will not be unhappy with him if you are sensible," the Prince replied, "and if you dig down into the past, trying to find out what happened before he knew you, you may easily make both of you very unhappy."

The Princess did not speak, and after a moment the Prince said in a more serious tone:

"I often think that the happiness we all seek is elusive and difficult to capture because we try to analyse it. We put it under a microscope, we prod and constrain it, so that it is difficult for it to expand and grow."

It was almost as if he spoke to himself, and Paulina knew exactly what he meant, but she could see that Margarita was bewildered.

"What His Royal Highness is saying," she said quickly, "is that you will be much happier if you believe what the Grand Duke says to you and if you give him your love as he is giving you his. What you have to do is to make sure that the future is yours and forget the past."

"But . . . if there is somebody special to whom he is attached . . ." the Princess began.

"If she was as special as that, he would be marrying her and not you," the Prince said quickly.

He saw that his sister was about to reply to him and went on:

"Margarita, my dear, do have some common sense. Alexander is in love with you—I am sure of that. The Tsar has approved the marriage, which is a great compliment to Altauss. There is nothing to be gained by worrying about other women or other attachments which are now in the past and should be forgotten."

Because he spoke quite sharply, tears came into the Princess's eyes and she jumped to her feet.

"I think you are being horrid and unsympathetic!" she said angrily. "It is not you, nor Paulina, who has to be married, but me! I am frightened—yes—I am frightened! And—neither of you—understands!"

Her voice broke on the last word and she ran across the *Boudoir* to pull open the door leading to her room and went through it, slamming it behind her.

Paulina rose to her feet.

"I must go to her," she said.

"No, wait a moment," the Prince answered. "I want to speak to you."

She looked at him a little apprehensively, wondering what he would say.

"Why does my sister feel like this?" he asked.

"I think it is understandable," Paulina replied. "When your father told her she was to be married, she could not even remember what her future husband looked like."

Prince Maximus frowned.

"I should have thought that the Grand Duke Alexander might have come and proposed to her in Altauss before she had to leave for St. Petersburg."

"That would have been more sensible and certainly kinder," Paulina agreed.

Prince Maximus sighed.

"It was obviously all arranged by the Tsar, and this is the way he always does things."

They were speaking in English, and Paulina said:

"Your sister is far more sensitive than most young women, and she is very young and inexperienced."

Quite unexpectedly the Prince smiled.

"You sound as if you were in your forties!"

"We are the same age," Paulina said, "but I admit at times to feeling very much older than the Princess because I have travelled so much and been with my father in so many different countries."

"And yet you are still very young."

Paulina gave a little laugh.

"There is no doubt that in a few years I shall grow older."

"Of course," he said, "but it will be a pity, because at the moment you look like spring itself, and that is something rare to find here in the Palace!"

He paused before he continued in a deep voice:

"In the exotic atmosphere of Russia everything grows too quickly, too exuberantly, and much, much too big."

Paulina laughed.

"That is what I think myself, especially where it concerns the buildings."

"I agree, so stay just as you are. But what are we to do about Margarita?"

"She will be all right," Paulina said, "as long as she is not upset by gossip as she has been now."

"Gossipping women!" the Prince exclaimed. "It is always the same! They are not only envious, jealous, and activated by malice—they cannot bear to see another woman happy."

"I think that is rather a sweeping generalisation," Paulina said. "But I love your sister and will do anything in my power to keep her happy."

She thought the Prince looked at her in a strange way, as if he was looking deep down into her soul to see if she was speaking the truth.

Then he said:

"I think that is true, but then you, Miss Handley, are exceptional, and I can only thank you for looking after Margarita in the way you are."

"The way I am . . . trying to do," Paulina corrected.

"I will leave you now," the Prince said. "Try to persuade Margarita to be reasonable, and I will speak to the Grand Duke, who I am sure is determined to make her happy."

"Please tell him how very young and inexperienced she is," Paulina pleaded. "As you know, she has never met anybody exactly like him before."

As she spoke she thought that she herself and never met anyone quite like Prince Maximus.

As she stood beside him, he was so tall that she had to tip her head back to look up at him.

He was overwhelming but not in the same way as the Russians were, and she knew it was because his Altauss blood made him much more human and sympathetic.

'I like him,' she thought to herself. 'There is something straight-forward and frank about him which is different from the Grand Duke or any of the other Russian men whom we have met here in St. Petersburg.'

Then she told herself that she was making up her mind too quickly and perhaps too conclusively.

At the same time, she knew that the Prince's concern for his sister and the way he was talking to her made her feel as if they were already friends.

"I promise you I will do everything I can," she said impulsively.

"I know you will do that," he answered in his deep voice.

She looked up into his eyes and felt as if she wanted to stay with him and to go on talking to him, even though she knew it was her duty to leave him and go to the Princess.

But just for a moment she could not move. Then she felt that without moving, without saying anything, the Prince held her.

With an effort that was surprisingly difficult, she dropped him a small curtsey and turned towards the door which led to the Princess's bed-chamber.

She reached it, but before she could turn the handle the Prince was there before her.

Then as she touched his hand she felt a strange vibration run through her fingers, and she knew with a sudden sensation of fear that Prince Maximus attracted her as no man had ever attracted her before.

* * *

The Prince had walked slowly down the stairs and was wending his way towards the Tsar's apartments when from an open door a hand, on whose wrist glittered a fabulous jewelled bracelet, came out to clutch his arm.

It was Princess Natasha, and she pulled him into one of the Ante-Chambers with which the Palace abounded, but which for the moment was empty.

It was lighted by candles in gold sconces on walls which were lined with books, and the Prince knew it was the sort of room used by those who brought petitions to the Tsar and were forced to sit for days, weeks, or even months before they received an audience.

"Where have you been?" Natasha asked.

"With my sister," the Prince replied.

"If she takes up too much of your time, I shall be jealous!"

"Of my sister?" he answered drily. "That is something quite new."

"I wondered where you had gone, and you must have known I wished to be with you."

"I thought you would be changing into something spectacular for the Ball."

The Prince spoke sarcastically, knowing that she could hardly possess a more spectacular gown than the one she was wearing at the moment, or finer jewels than those which glittered like a formation of stars or a small moon.

The Princess put her arms round his neck.

"Why are we wasting time, Maximus?" she asked.

"Kiss me, and later tonight when we can be alone together, I will tell you how much I have missed you."

She would have pulled his head towards her, but at that moment the door opened behind them and they both stiffened and the Princess's arms dropped to her sides.

Someone came into the room and they saw it was an elderly noble who Prince guessed was in search of somewhere he could rest for a while before the more arduous duties of the evening were thrust upon him.

He obviously did not recognise either of them, but bowing them a greeting moved across the room to lower himself carefully into one of the large armchairs beside the inevitable lighted stove which remained on at this particular time of the year.

The Princess's lips tightened.

"Curse the old fool!" she said beneath her breath. "Now I shall have to wait until the Ball ends and we can leave discreetly."

"It will certainly be difficult now," the Prince said.

"Then we will wait," she said, "but it will be hard."

She spoke softly, and without waiting for the Prince to reply she left the room and was moving swiftly along the passage before he could follow her.

As the Prince walked towards the Salon there was a serious expression on his face and he appeared to be deep in thought.

He went in search of the Grand Duke Alexander and found him, as he had expected, in a room used by the Tsar's guests who were gathered there while the ladies rested and changed their gowns between dinner supper.

The Grand Duke was drinking champagne and laughing with two gorgeously arrayed officers of the Imperial Guard who both rose to their feet as Prince Maximus approached.

He smiled at them and said:

"Will you gentlemen forgive me while I have a few

words alone with the Grand Duke? As you are well aware, it is always very difficult to have a quiet conversation in this Palace, where far too many people are housed."

They laughed, and one of the officers said:

"How can we refuse Your Royal Highness when you have fought with such distinction against a man who has defied us for nearly forty years?"

"We have still not won the battle," Prince Maximus replied, "and I would like to say that I have the greatest admiration and respect for Shamyl. His courage is unbelievable, and his tenacity is something we can well emulate."

"I do not believe you," the second of the officers said, "and quite frankly, I have no wish to be sent to the Caucasus. I have heard too much of the hardship you have endured there."

Then the two officers walked away and the Prince sat down beside the Grand Duke.

"Peacetime soldiers!" he said scornfully.

"They had better not let the Tsar hear them say that," the Grand Duke replied, "or they will find themselves in the front line in the next battle."

"Do them good!" the Prince said. "Our men in the Caucasus have been outstandingly brave, and I can assure you it is very difficult for them, meeting tactics quite unknown in any other campaign the Russians have fought."

"Meanwhile, it has taken them forty years, and you, to get as far as they have now," the Grand Duke said.

"You flatter me," the Prince said, "but honestly, Alexander, I sometimes feel that those living in luxury here and toasting our efforts have no idea what is happening on battlefields that are red with blood."

"It is quite useless for you to try to make them

understand," the Grand Duke said, "so let us talk about something more pleasing."

"My sister, for example," Prince Maximus said.

The Grand Duke looked up at the Prince.

"Has anything upset her?"

"Only that she has heard some gossip which has frightened her."

"Those cackling women! It happens the world over," the Grand Duke said, "and there is nothing mere men can do about it."

"Except to reassure her," Prince Maximus said.

"How can I do that?"

"By making her believe that your past is past and the future is hers."

The Grand Duke sighed.

"I know exactly what you are saying to me, Maximus, but it is not easy."

There was silence and the Prince waited, thinking that the Grand Duke was about to say more—something he perhaps thought he ought to know.

Then unexpectedly the Grand Duke said:

"Thank you for telling me what I ought to have known, but as the Tsar decided our marriage should take place at the end of next week, I am quite certain I shall be able to manage in my own way."

"All I ask is that you try to make Margarita happy," the Prince said.

The Grand Duke smiled.

"That is what I intend to do. I love her, Maximus, and I intend that we shall both be very happy together. She is very lovely and very young, and she is different from all the women here, who are coquettish and start living lives of their own before they have even left the cradle."

Prince Maximus laughed.

"I know exactly what you mean, but do remember that Russian ways and Russian ideas are different from those of any other country in the world."

"I will remember that," the Grand Duke said. "At the same time, you seem to have forgotten quite easily."

"I enjoy being here," the Prince said quietly. "I am extremely grateful to the Tsar for the position he has given me in your Army and for the favours he has heaped on me. At the same time, I find many things alien and a little difficult to swallow, so to speak."

The Prince looked sharply at the man sitting beside him before he added:

"It is difficult for me, but you can understand it will be much more difficult for a woman, especially one as young as Margarita, who has lived a very closeted life in a simple, uncomplicated, friendly country."

"Again I understand what you are saying to me," the Grand Duke replied, "and I can only say that I intend to make your sister happy, as I am happy that she is to be my wife."

Again the Prince had the uneasy feeling that the Grand Duke was keeping something back.

It was something he could not quite put his finger on, and yet the impression was there.

The Grand Duke held out his hand.

"Thank you, Maximus. I am delighted to have you here. We have not seen a great deal of each other. At the same time, I think we have what the French call a sympathy that is undeniable."

The Prince put his hand in his.

"All I can say is that if my sister is to marry a Russian," he said, "then I would rather it was you than anybody else."

"Thank you, Maximus! Thank you for a two-edged compliment! It is a good thing the Tsar does not hear it!"

"I agree with you," Maximus said with a smile. "He would not understand."

Chapter Four

The Ball-Room was even lovelier than Paulina had expected.

She had heard so often of how the Tsar changed Ball-Rooms into gardens and gardens into fantastic Palaces.

Sometimes as many as three thousand workmen were employed to produce rockeries and fountains inside the house.

She thought now that the Ball-Room was a perfect setting for the peacock uniforms designed by the Tsar, while the gigantic mirrors reflected the brilliance of the jewels sparkling and shimmering as the ladies spun and dipped to the music of innumerable violins.

Although she had been to a number of Balls in Altauss and one or two in Italy before she had really grown up, this surpassed anything she had ever seen or imagined.

She had felt as if she had stepped into a fairy-tale Ballet where everyone was beautiful and had a grace that had nothing to do with the mundane, everyday existence of ordinary people.

Amongst all the women she watched moving over the polished floor, she could not prevent her eyes from going continually towards Princess Natasha.

She had seemed fantastic at dinner, and now she appeared to glitter with all the exotic brilliance of the Orient.

66

Huge emeralds spilled over her breast to her waist, emeralds sparkled in her hair and on her wrists, and as she moved round the room with Prince Maximus, Paulina thought no couple could look more outstanding.

Princess Margarita was dancing continually with her fiancé and Paulina found herself partnered by a number of handsome *Aides-de-Camp* and officers who paid her extravagant compliments.

They would have made her shy if she had not heard much the same remarks from dark-eyed and vivacious Italians.

Beyond the Ball-Room there were other rooms literally transformed into gardens of flowers and it was impossible to believe that one was not really out-of-doors.

Even the ceilings had been painted blue with glowing lights in them to glitter like stars, and there were great banks of roses, lilies, orchids and carnations, which scented the air until their fragrance was almost overpowering.

"You are very beautiful, *Mademoiselle*," Paulina's partner said to her. "The moment I saw you, my heart leapt in my breast, and I knew I had fallen precipitately and irrevocably in love."

Paulina, laughing lightly, answered in French:

"You are very flattering, *Monsieur*, but I find it hard to believe you are sincere."

The Russian clasped his hand over hers as he said:

"I swear to you on my life that every word I say is true, and I shall spend the next thousand years trying to make you believe me."

Paulina laughed again.

"You are cruel and heartless," he protested. "Surely you know when a man speaks the truth! I indeed mean every word I say! That we should meet was written in the sands of fate."

"Everything you say sounds unreal, just as what I see round me is unreal too," Paulina answered.

For a moment her partner looked disconcerted, then he replied:

"May I say you are being very English? Only the English can be matter-of-fact over things which are too imaginative to be put into words."

"I think that perhaps 'sensible' would be a better word."

He looked at Paulina and moved a little nearer as he said:

"I love you and I promise one day you will love me."

She thought it was tiresome to argue with him. Instead she said:

"It is very warm here. Would it be possible for me to have something to drink?"

"Of course," her partner replied. "I should have thought of it before. I will summon a servant."

He rose from where they were sitting by a bank of crimson roses which were so skilfully arranged that they looked as if they had grown and come into blossom all at the same time.

As he left, Paulina gave a little sigh of relief.

All her partners so far had been nearly as ardent as this one.

She knew, although she had forgotten their names, that they were of great social importance, and while they would offer her their hearts they certainly would not offer her a wedding-ring.

Not that she was looking for a husband.

She had already made up her mind that her father need not worry about her, because however handsome, eloquent, and charming the Russians might be, she had no wish to marry one.

The thought of marriage conjured up questions as if they were spoken by someone else, and in answer she heard a woman's voice behind the roses ask:

"What do you think of the little Princess from Altauss?"

"I think she is lovely, and Alexander is a lucky man," a man replied. "The Tsar could have chosen someone very different for him."

"She was the Tsar's choice?"

"I imagine so."

"I suppose," the lady said, "he thought it a mistake for Alexander to go on as he was. Most liaisons of that sort do not last so long."

"Marie-Celeste was rather different. She was very attractive and he was for many years completely faithful to her."

"Frenchwomen are very clever at holding their men," the lady remarked scornfully. "What has happened to her now?"

"I believe she has gone back to France, taking her son with her, although the Tsar promised that he would be responsible for him."

Paulina held in her breath. She felt as if what she was hearing could not be true.

Yet, she knew that it was. This was the secret that Margarita had guessed and which she too had felt was hidden in the Grand Duke's past.

She clasped her hands together as she waited for the couple, whom she could not see, to say something more.

Then the lady said in a bored tone:

"With Alexander married, we will have nothing to gossip about. It will be up to you, Vladimir, to amuse us!"

"You may be sure I shall do my best," the gentleman replied.

It was then that Paulina's partner returned, accompanied by a servant carrying a gold tray on which was a variety of drinks.

Paulina picked up a glass, hardly aware of what she was doing.

She was shattered by what she had just heard, knowing that if Margarita had been in her place and had overheard the conversation, it would have destroyed the love which like the first buds of spring was beginning to appear in her feelings towards the Grand Duke.

What Paulina said to her partner afterwards she later had no idea.

She knew only that it was a relief to go back to the Ball-Room to dance with somebody else and try to sort out in her own mind what she should do or say.

What she was afraid of was that some of the chattering women, which included almost everyone she had met so far, would tell Margarita that the Grand Duke had a son by another woman and that they had been for years to all intents and purposes married.

"If he loved her so much, why did he not marry her?" Paulina asked herself, and was aware that it was a stupid question to which she knew the answer.

No member of the Royal Family could marry without the permission of the Tsar, and as she had learnt from her father, most marriages were decided by him and there was no question of any appeal against his decision.

"At least the Frenchwoman has gone away," she told herself.

She was sure that in consequence everything would be all right in the future, unless Margarita learnt how much she had meant to the Grand Duke and that she had given him a son.

Because she herself was so innocent about love, she was in fact very shocked that a gentleman should have a permanent liaison which resulted in children.

She could not have lived in diplomatic circles without knowing that there were Courtesans in every country, on whom men expended large sums of money and who wore their jewellery as if they were medals won in battle.

But they were very different from the ladies who pursued her father. Although she knew that he spent time with some of them and because he was so handsome they obviously wished to kiss him, Paulina had no idea how a man and woman actually made love to each other.

Vaguely she thought it must be something very wonderful if it made her father and mother as happy as they had been together.

She also believed that children were the result of love and therefore were inevitable when one was married.

That the Grand Duke should have had a son without being married both surprised and shocked her.

The more she thought about it, the more she felt it was a menace to Margarita's happiness and could rock the whole foundation on which her marriage rested.

'I must speak to the Prince, I must speak to the Prince!' she thought.

But it was impossible to get near him, for every time she thought there was a chance to speak to him, Princess Natasha was at his side, holding on to his arm and looking up at him in a manner which Paulina knew her mother would have thought fast and immodest.

Only when it was very late, or rather early in the morning, and several of the older guests were yawning behind their hands did the Tsar dance with Princess Natasha.

As Paulina watched them take the floor she was aware that somebody had come to her side.

"May I have this dance, Miss Handley?" Prince Maximus asked, and she turned towards him eagerly.

"I want to speak to you!" she said as they took the first steps of a waltz.

"I shall be delighted to listen," he replied, "but first I want to dance with you, because you are, as I suspected, as light as thistle-down."

He was speaking English and Paulina could not help giving a little laugh.

"How do you know about English thistle-down?" she enquired.

"I suspect we have some in Altauss," he replied, "but if you prefer, I will compare you to a firefly or perhaps a lark flying high into the sky."

Paulina laughed again.

"You are as poetical as the Russians."

"They have been teaching me that I have been much too 'backward in coming forward,' as my Nanny used to say."

Paulina looked surprised.

"So you had an English Nanny!"

"Of course, they are very *comme il faut* in Altauss, just as here in Russia they not only have English Nannies but a profusion of French tutors."

"I heard that French was all the rage," Paulina said.

"I assure you," he replied, "nobody ranks as fashionable if they do not possess at least one foreign import, French or English, and that is why you will find that with such instructors we all eventually become mongrels in our characters and personalities."

It was impossible not to laugh at what he was saying, but all the time Paulina was thinking of what she had overheard.

After they had danced round the room a number of times she looked up at him appealingly and he knew without words what she was asking.

He swung her round once again, her skirts billowing out like the sails of a ship at sea.

Then skilfully, in what she felt was a way of disappearing without drawing attention to themselves, he moved her not into the room made to look like a garden where she had been before, but into another.

Here small arbours had been constructed and the only light came from an artificial moon which hovered above them.

It threw no light into the arbours themselves, which made the darkness very inviting to those who wished to be alone and unnoticed.

Paulina sat down on a cushioned sofa and she could only just vaguely see the Prince's face as he sat next to her.

As he turned towards her his arm was on the back of the sofa.

"Now, what is worrying you?" he asked.

Paulina drew in her breath, then hesitatingly, a little shy at what she had to say, she told him what she had overheard.

When her voice died into silence he did not speak, and after some moments had passed she said accusingly:

"You knew of this?"

"Yes, I knew about it."

"And you do not think it ... wrong for your sister to ... marry a man who has a ... child by another . . . woman?"

Again there was silence. Then the Prince said unexpectedly:

"I am surprised that my father did not think it a mistake to send Margarita to Russia with somebody as young and unsophisticated as you."

Paulina stiffened.

"Are you saying that I am not the right person to be a Lady-in-Waiting to the Princess?"

"What I am thinking is that perhaps an older woman would be able to accept such things and would certainly not be shocked as you are."

"You may consider such behaviour of no importance, but I am thinking of your sister."

"I, too, am thinking of her," the Prince said, "and I assure you, Miss Handley, that I meant what I said tonight in all sincerity. The past is past, and Margarita's future lies with a man who will love and look after her and perhaps be able to do so far better because he has had some experience of women."

"But ... he has a son!" Paulina murmured beneath her breath. "And it is ... wrong that he should not have ... married the ... mother of his child."

"That is something that, however regrettable, occurs continually, not only in modern life but all through history."

"I am . . . aware of . . . that," Paulina said. "At the same time . . . if your sister learns of it, how can she ever be . . . happy?"

She paused before she went on in a low voice:

"Perhaps the Grand Duke will long to see his son, to be with him, to teach him all the things a man wants to teach a small . . . replica of . . . himself."

As she spoke she was thinking how bitterly her father always regretted that he had only a daughter.

Once her mother had said to her:

"You have to make up, my darling, to Papa for the fact that I was unable to give him the son he wanted so much."

"Why should he want a boy more than a girl?" Paulina had asked defiantly.

"Because," her mother had replied with a smile, "to all men it is something that matters more than anything else that they should have sons and teach them to ride, to shoot, to follow in their footsteps, and of course to continue the family name."

Paulina had been very young at the time, and because she loved her father she was jealous that he should want a boy and not her.

"Why can I not be enough for Papa?" she had asked.

"Because, darling, although Papa loves you very much," her mother had replied, "you are a girl, and one day you will marry and take your husband's name and give him a son! Then your family will not be ours but his."

Paulina had tried to understand the difference, and as she grew older there were innumerable occasions when she knew her father was wishing that he had a son to follow him into the Diplomatic Service as well as in the field of sport.

She herself would have loved to have a brother as handsome, charming, and companionable as her father was, but of her own age.

As she thought of it, she knew that if she were marrying a man who had a son by another wife, or by his mistress, she would feel that she had been deprived and defrauded.

She would want desperately to give him something that was very special and precious to them both, but especially to him.

As if he followed her thoughts, the Prince said quietly:

"However much we may regret it, we cannot undo the past."

"And yet, knowing this, you thought the Grand Duke was the right husband for the Princess?"

"Actually I was not consulted on the matter," Prince Maximus admitted, "but if I had been, I would not have thought it an insurmountable obstacle to Margarita's happiness."

"It would be to me," Paulina said without thinking.

"But you are not Royal," the Prince replied, "and as your father's daughter you know as well as I do that there is one law for us and another for those who have the responsibility of ruling."

"If this is what happens, then I am deeply sorry for you," Paulina said.

"I suspect we are often sorry for ourselves," the Prince said. "At the same time, Margarita will find many advantages in being a Grand Duchess and part of the Tsar's family. He may be difficult and a tyrant towards the country at large, but to his family he is protective and on the whole loving."

This Paulina was prepared to believe, having heard the same thing from her father. At the same time, she was still worried.

"What you have to do," the Prince said almost sharply, "is to make certain that these gossiping, tittle-

tattling women do not upset Margarita, and I am very
thankful that she was not in your place tonight."

"So am I!" Paulina said fervently.

"I am also sorry," he said softly, "that it should
upset you."

"As you have already said, it is only because I
am . . . inexperienced and unsophisticated."

"You are both those things," he agreed, "which is
why I think it was a mistake for you to come to Russia.
It is a strange, wild, very exciting country, but dangerous in many ways for somebody like yourself."

"I am not afraid personally," Paulina replied, "and
Papa warned me what Russia was like."

"By that I presume you mean he warned you
against Russian men," the Prince said. "So listen to me,
I beg of you."

There was a note in his voice that made her look at
his in surprise, and he said quietly:

"You are very beautiful, and it is inevitable that a
great number of men will tell you so. But you must
remember that they cannot marry without the Tsar's
permission, and he would never allow anyone who had
Royal blood in their veins to marry a commoner."

He spoke very slowly and seriously, and Paulina
replied quickly:

"I am aware of that, and what you mean is that it
would have been impossible for the Grand Duke to
have married the French lady even morganatically."

The Prince nodded his head.

"She came from a good French family. Her father
was not one of the great Aristocrats but was still a
gentleman. Yet, His Imperial Majesty would not have
considered her suitable in any way for the Grand Duke."

Paulina pressed her lips together.

She wanted to say: "In that case, the Grand Duke
should have left her alone and she should not have
allowed herself to be persuaded into such a position."

Then the Prince said softly:

"Love is stronger than caution or commonsense, and there is no doubt that the Grand Duke was for many years happy with somebody who loved him for himself and not for his social position."

"And now?" Paulina asked.

"It is over, completely and absolutely over, and I am assured by his friends, although he has not discussed it with me personally, that he will not see the lady again."

"That is . . . something in his favour," Paulina said almost beneath her breath.

The Prince did not answer for a moment. Then after what seemed a long pause he said:

"I understand that arrangements have been made about the boy, but it is not our business, and what we have to do, you and I, Paulina, is to prevent Margarita from ever knowing of his existence."

Because he spoke so seriously, Paulina hardly noticed that he had used her Christian name, and because she was thinking only of the Princess she answered eagerly:

"Will you speak to the Grand Duke? Will you explain to him how important it is that Margarita should not know?"

"Yes, I will speak to him."

"I know you think it . . . foolish of me to be . . . upset by what I have . . . heard," Paulina said hesitatingly, "but because I am upset . . . I know . . . exactly how the Princess would feel. It may be . . . difficult for the Grand Duke to understand that because she is not Russian, her . . . reaction would be different from that of a girl who has been brought up in the Royal circle in this country."

To her surprise, the Prince reached out, took her hand, and lifted it to his lips.

"When you told me tonight," he said quietly, "that you would look after Margarita and try to keep her happy, I hoped you were speaking the truth. Now I

know how much she means to you, and I am more
grateful than I can express in words."

He kissed her hand again, and the touch of his lips
against her skin gave Paulina a strange feeling.

She had often had her hand kissed before, but this
was somehow different, although she could not explain
why.

"Now I must take you back to the Ball-Room," the
Prince said. "If we stay here any longer, the gossips will
be talking about us, and that, I am sure, would be a
mistake."

"Yes . . . of course," Paulina said quickly.

She felt she had somehow been at fault in staying
so long, but she knew she had to talk to him about the
Princess.

She rose to her feet, and as she stepped out of the
arbour the light from the artificial moon was on her and
enveloped her in silver.

It made her look very young and at the same time
insubstantial and ethereal, as if like the moonlight she
came from somewhere outside in the Heavens.

She looked up at the Prince and found he was
looking at her. His eyes were very dark, and yet they
seemed magnetic as they held hers captive in a way she
could not explain.

For a moment it was impossible to move.

Then in a little voice that seemed somehow lost in
a strange world, Paulina said:

"We . . . must . . . go."

"Yes, of course," the Prince agreed, as if he had
not thought of it before.

In silence they walked towards the music coming
from the Ball-Room.

*   *   *

Dawn was already creeping up the sky when the
Prince finally reached his bedroom.

A tired valet was awaiting up for him to help him out of his elaborate tunic.

The Prince did not speak. He merely undressed, put on a long robe which reached to the ground, and walked to the window to draw back the curtains.

The first rays of the rising sun were touching the domes of the Churches on the other side of the river, and there was nobody about.

The whole world seemed very quiet and still.

It was then that he remembered the message in Natasha's eyes as a little earlier she had said good-night and left the Ball-Room.

He knew that as soon as his valet left she would come to his room through one of the secret entrances, which were to be found in almost every bedroom in the Winter Palace, if one knew where to look for them.

He was sure that Natasha had been made aware of them by the Third Section or perhaps by the Tsar himself.

Although he had never questioned it to himself before, he thought now that it was wrong that she should approach him rather than he approach her.

In all his *affaires de coeur,* and there had been a great number in his life, it was the women who waited for him, not he for the women.

Quite suddenly the Prince felt that he was being manipulated and it was something he disliked.

Intensely masculine, he wanted to be master, he wanted to conquer the woman he desired, he wanted her to surrender to him.

Now he thought that when Natasha approached him she would be like an animal stalking its prey, sure of herself, confident that she would satisfy her desires and he would not resist her.

It was wrong, it was against nature and against his own inclinations.

He was also aware that the fire that had burnt so fiercely between them the last time they had been together in St. Petersburg had not been ignited tonight when they danced together.

Nor had it flared into flame when she had spoken to him in a manner which in the past would have made him vibrate irresistibly towards her.

As the sun was sweeping away the last stars from the sky, the Prince made up his mind, and as the valet left the room with his evening-clothes over his arm and with a respectful "good-night," he drew back the curtains over the window.

Giving the man just enough time to pass down the passage into the shadows at the end of it, the Prince opened the door and went from the room.

He had stayed so often in the Palace that he knew it well.

He was aware that on this floor there were a number of bedrooms usually allotted to the Tsar's guests who were Royal enough to be housed in State-Rooms but who did not require very spacious accommodation if they had come without their wives.

As there were not very many guests in this particular party, Prince Maximus knew that at least six of the rooms in this part of the Palace would be empty.

He walked a little way down the passage and, relying on his instinct and a belief in his luck, chose a door at random and opened it.

The room inside was in darkness, and he paused for a moment, listening for the sound of breathing coming from the bed.

Reassured by a silence that seemed almost oppressive, he crossed the room towards the window, guided by the faint light that came from between the drawn curtains.

As he pulled them back he turned quickly and saw as he had expected that not only was the bed empty, but the covers had not been taken from it.

With a faint smile on his lips, Prince Maximus walked back to the door and locked it, then returned to

the bed and threw off the heavy silk cover embroidered
with the Imperial Coat-of-Arms.

Then, taking off his robe, he slipped between the
sheets and settled himself down preparatory to sleep.

He was aware that in the morning he would somehow have to deal with Natasha and make some plausible
explanation for his absence.

He was not certain what this would be, but, confident that he would think of something to say, he slept
peacefully.

* * *

Paulina and the Princess had retired to bed somewhat earlier, since the Princess was tired and ready to
leave the Ball-Room.

As the two girls went up the wide staircase together the Princess said:

"It has been such an exciting evening! I had no
idea that Alexander could dance so well—far better
than anyone else I have ever danced with."

"Your brother is also a good dancer," Paulina said.

"I saw you dancing with him," the Princess replied,
"and I was glad he could escape for the moment from
that emerald-eyed houri, Princess Natasha! I hate her!"

Paulina looked at the Princess in surprise.

"But you hardly know her," she said. "What has
she done to upset you?"

"You must have seen the way she was behaving
with Maximus," Margarita replied. "I think she should
be ashamed of being so blatantly vulgar. It is not what I
expected in an Imperial Ball-Room."

Paulina had thought the same herself, but she
knew it would be a mistake to say so.

"The Princess is very . . . beautiful in an . . . Oriental
way," she said slowly.

"I suppose Maximus admires her, but I cannot
think why," the Princess said, "and from all I have

heard about the Princess Natasha, she is a wicked woman!"

"Why should you say that?" Paulina asked.

The Princess put her lips near to Paulina's ear as she said:

"She spies for the Tsar! One of the ladies was telling me tonight that when he wants to find out something from Diplomats like your father, the Princess entices them into giving away the secrets of their country."

"Is that true?" Paulina asked in astonishment.

"That is what the woman told me," Margarita answered. "She said she and some of the other Royal hostesses would like to exclude her from their parties, but as she is useful to the Tsar there is nothing they can do about it."

Paulina thought Princess Natasha's behaviour had been strange, especially the way she had flirted with Prince Maximus, and now she asked:

"Do you think your . . . brother knows . . . this about . . . her?"

"I expect so," Margarita said lightly, "but if she is pretty enough to attract him, Maximus will not worry about her being a spy. After all, he has no secrets to hide."

That was easy to say, but as a Diplomat's daughter Paulina thought there might be quite a number of secrets in Altauss that it would be dangerous for the Tsar, or the head of any other country, to know and be able to use to his own advantage.

"If what you say is true," she said, "I think your brother should be warned."

As she spoke she knew that she hated the idea of the Prince being used by somebody like Princess Natasha and perhaps unwarily stepping into a trap which might result in a scandal or an accusation of what his own countrymen might think of as treachery.

Then she remembered that her father had said so often that no Diplomat could afford to be indiscreet!

Secondly, Paulina thought it was a mistake for Prince Maximus to associate with someone who might, without his being aware of it, extract information which could be used by the Third Section!

Hardly being aware of it, she said a quick prayer that Prince Maximus might be safe!

After she had said good-night to Margarita and gone to her own room, she had lain thinking about him and the beautiful Princess Natasha.

'I suppose she is the sort of woman he finds attractive,' she thought.

She knew how dull and insignificant she herself must look beside a woman who had the grace of a gazelle combined with the feline strength of a wild animal.

Because Paulina was perceptive, she could almost understand that someone like Princess Natasha would be attractive to a man simply because she was different from any other woman.

There was a mystery about her and a magnetism which Paulina knew in her heart was wrong and evil! The Prince was good, but because the Princess was subtle he might not be aware of what she was really like.

'I must warn him,' she thought.

Then she knew it was something she could not ever do, and he would doubtless think her extremely impertinent and intrusive if she did.

"Please, God, save him, please . . . please . . ." she prayed in the darkness.

Then frighteningly, like a whisper relentlessly in her ear, she wondered if Princess Natasha meant the same to the Prince as the Frenchwoman, Marie-Celeste, had meant to the Grand Duke.

"No, no, no!" something within her cried out at the idea.

Yet, because she had no answer to the question, unexpectedly Paulina felt that she wanted to cry.

*   *   *

The next day there was the bustling confusion of the whole Court moving to Tsarskoe-Selo.

From the moment Paulina and the Princess awoke, their rooms seemed to be full of servants packing, chattering, and asking for orders.

There were great leather trunks being dragged out to the passages once they were ready, and endless discussions of what first the Princess and then Paulina would wear.

When finally they went downstairs, it was to find that the confusion was the same below as it had been above.

It seemed strange, considering that the Tsar and the Tsarina were regularly travelling backwards and forwards to their Summer Palace, which was actually little more than an hour-and-a-half's drive from St. Petersburg.

Paulina was delighted to find that they were to drive in open carriages from the Palace and the Grand Duke was to accompany them.

With her back to the horses, she was able to see the open country through which they passed, which was flat and not very interesting, although quite a number of trees had been planted, which being now in blossom looked exceedingly attractive.

She could not help noticing, however, that many of the people they passed on the road were in rags and were very dirty in appearance.

It seemed a poignant contrast to the smart and luxurious appearance of the carriages with their well-groomed horses, and with the coachmen's uniforms, chosen by the Tsar, being so ornate and fantastic as to be almost fancy-dress.

The Grand Duke talked quietly to Margarita for

most of the journey, and Paulina tactfully tried not to overhear what he was saying and turned her face towards the countryside so that they could feel as if they were alone.

She still found it impossible not to think about the Frenchwoman with whom the Grand Duke had lived for so many years.

She could not help wondering again what would happen if Margarita learnt of his son, and if so, whether she might at the last moment refuse to marry him.

Then she told herself that there was no possibility of the Princess doing such a thing, and even if she tried now to break the engagement she would be forced into marriage both by her father and by the Tsar.

"She is really only a puppet manipulated for the good of Altauss," Paulina said to herself, "and that country is very grateful for the generosity of Imperial Russia."

Her lips tightened as she added:

"It is all politics!"

She hated the idea that Margarita, whom she loved, should be involved in the cold-blooded schemes of Statesmen.

However, there was nothing she could do but try to ensure that Margarita should never learn of something which would distress her, even though Prince Maximus might think she was absurd to make such a fuss about it.

Tsarskoe-Selo was a beautiful building surrounded by magnificent gardens brilliant with flowers.

As soon as they arrived they were informed that there was quite a small party at the Palace at the moment and Prince Maximus was one of the guests.

Looking down the list which one of the Courtiers held in his hand, Paulina saw with delight that Princess Natasha's name was not included.

When she could not find the name that she dreaded, something heavy that had lain on her breast all the

morning lightened, while the sunshine seemed brighter
and the Palace itself more brilliant than it had looked
before.

Then as they reached the magnificent and very
pretty Suite of rooms which had been allotted to the
Princess, Paulina said as if she could not keep the good
news to herself:

"Princess Natasha is not staying here, so you will
be able to see more of your brother than you would
have done otherwise."

"Oh, good!" Margarita exclaimed. "If he is not
being bewitched by that ghastly woman and is paying
attention to us, there will be no-one more fun than
Maximus!"

As the maid carried away her travelling-cape and
the very pretty bonnet she had worn, she added to
Paulina:

"I am so happy because Alexander said such delightful things to me in the carriage, and did you see
that he was holding my hand?"

"Yes, I saw that," Paulina answered.

"He loves me for myself," Margarita said. "I am
sure that I am beginning to fall very much in love with
him."

"Oh, dearest, I am so glad!" Paulina cried.

"I do not really mind being married so quickly,"
Margarita went on, "and Alexander says I may rearrange
all his Palace and do things exactly the way I want to,
including having dinner at a reasonable hour and not
having to go back to bed afterwards."

Paulina laughed and kissed the Princess.

"I am sure if you look so pretty and coax the Grand
Duke, you can get everything you want."

"Do you remember what Papa told us once? That
'one catches more flies with honey than with vinegar'!"

Paulina laughed. She remembered it well.

Margarita had been storming at one of the servants

for doing something wrong and the Grand Duke Louis had heard her.

He had taken both girls into his Study and given them a lecture on being pleasant to those beneath them.

"Woman who are pretty can get their own way by smiling and being charming," he had said. "It is far easier and far quicker than using any other method. Always remember that."

Paulina had told her father what the Grand Duke had said, and Sir Christopher had exclaimed:

"I thought you knew that already! You have only to follow your mother's example. She could twist anybody round her finger—man, woman, or child—just by using her charm."

"I will try to do the same," Paulina had said.

"You do it already, my dearest," Sir Christopher had answered with a smile, "and I find it hard to say 'no' to anything you ask of me."

Because Princess Margarita was so pretty and had a child-like way of asking for favours, Paulina was quite certain that it was what the Grand Duke would appreciate.

Then insidiously the question slipped into her mind as to how Marie-Celeste had asked for things, and she wondered too what Princess Natasha's attitude was towards Prince Maximus when they were alone together.

Because she did not want to think of it, she quickly talked of other things.

She made Margarita laugh at some of the compliments she had been paid the night before, and added how extravagant she thought it was to have such elaborate decorations and gardens constructed in the Winter Palace when they were all leaving the next day.

The Princess shrugged her shoulders.

"What does it matter?" she asked. "The Tsar is a very rich man."

"But the people we have seen beside the roads look very, very poor," Paulina protested.

The Princess did not seem interested, and it occurred to Paulina that it would be a mistake for her to make Margarita too aware of the contrast between poverty and luxury which she had noticed since she came to Russia.

The Princess would have to live here, and Paulina knew it would upset her every day to think of people suffering from starvation and the intense cold of the winters when so much money was thrown away on luxuries in the Palaces.

'If I lived here I would want to do something about the poor,' she thought, and shrank with a physical pain from the idea of living in Russia permanently.

Then she knew that most people would think only that the grandeur, the opulence, and the excitement made it very thrilling.

'Perhaps when Prince Maximus goes back to Altauss to reign,' she thought, 'when his father dies, he will find that dear little country dull and unexciting after the life he has lived here.'

It had not occurred to her before, but now she thought perhaps it was a mistake that the Grand Duke had allowed his son to leave the country of his origin and become important in the Russian Army and a favourite of the Tsar.

It might have imbued him with the grandiose ideas of the Russians, which included their wild excesses and apparently a complete disregard for the sufferings of the serfs whom they owned, body and soul, while the ordinary people crept about, hungry and in rags.

"It is wrong! It is wrong!" Paulina told herself.

She wondered if she would be brave enough to discuss it with Prince Maximus and knew it was something she must not do.

"I must not presume on my position," she told herself.

But she knew it was her English blood which made her long for justice and her English upbringing which made her want to consider those who were dependent on her family.

She knew how careful her father had been before he left England to ensure that the old people who had served him and his father before him were looked after in his absence.

He owned what was only a small Estate in Buckinghamshire, but the Manor House had been in the Handley family for three hundred years, and because her mother had loved it, Paulina loved it too.

Sir Christopher's diplomatic life meant they were more often away than at home, but it was there—a place of refuge and security when the time came for him to retire.

To Paulina, of all the many other houses she had lived in, the Manor was always "home."

'We would never let our old people suffer as the Russians let theirs,' she thought.

She felt she was gradually accumulating in her mind ideas of Russia which made her admire some of the things she had seen so far but also forced her to deprecate a lot of others.

"England is so small by comparison," she murmured beneath her breath.

Then, thinking of Altauss, she felt it was a happy, uncomplicated land, enveloped with sunshine.

She could see her father riding across the Park towards the Palace, walking through the woods with his gun, sitting reading in the comfortable Library in the Legation or in the garden filled with English flowers.

'That is the simple life I want to live,' she decided.

Then just by looking out the window she could see the fountains playing, the ornamental figures on the terrace encrusted with gold leaf, and a garden filled with exotic flowers.

It was beautiful but artificial, and she felt that

England and Altauss were very different, so different that she knew that very shortly she would be counting the days until she could return to her father's side.

Then as she thought of it, unmistakably and insistently the picture came to her mind of the Prince as she had seen him last, his eyes looking down at her as they stood beneath the artificial moon amidst the flower-filled arbours.

She had known as she looked up at him that something passed between them which she could not explain.

Yet, it vibrated like some magnetic alarm, and was at the same time like the sound of music and as untouchable as a star.

Paulina drew in her breath.

"I must not think about him," she said to herself. "It is dangerous when he is so far out of reach! He will become a Ruler, and because of it he will marry a Royal Princess who has been chosen for him by the Tsar!"

Chapter Five

Walking in the garden, Paulina felt lonely.

She had slipped away from the Palace, knowing she was not wanted. The flowers, brilliant in the sunshine, made her feel homesick for Altauss.

She wished she were brave enough to suggest that she should go home since it was quite obvious that even her usefulness to the Princess had come to an end.

The day after they had arrived at Tsarskoe-Selo, the Grand Duke's three sisters arrived and made such a fuss of Margarita that Paulina felt they almost elbowed her out of their way.

The sisters were all young, very attractive, and very vivacious.

It was obvious that they welcomed their brother's marriage enthusiastically, and Paulina felt secretly that they were relieved to be rid of the Frenchwoman to whom he had been attached for so long.

Margarita, always responsive to kindness and affection, was growing daily more and more in love with her future husband, and she found his sisters enchanting.

"How lucky I am," she said to Paulina, "to have such charming in-laws. I have always been afraid that the relations of any man I married would resent me and, if they were women, would perhaps be a little jealous."

The three sisters complimented Margarita and convinced her that the marriage not only had their approv-

91

al but that all the Grand Duke's other relations were delighted that he was to be married.

They brought with them the most fantastic jewels as presents, and Margarita arrayed herself in them not only when they were there but when she was alone with Paulina.

There was a set of sapphires that was particularly becoming, especially the tiara, which was large enough to be a crown, while Paulina thought the necklace of diamonds must be worth a King's ransom.

"How could I imagine," Margarita asked in awe-struck tones, "that I would ever own anything so excitingly beautiful?"

Paulina was sure that the Princess was exactly the wife that the Vladirvitches had wanted for the head of their family, and it was possible to express their gratitude and relief at the marriage only by giving the bride extravagant and luxurious presents.

One was a cape of sables which was as fine as anything owned by the Tsarina, besides other furs which would be very necessary for Margarita to wear when the winds from Siberia brought the intense cold to St. Petersburg, which everyone dreaded.

'I shall be home by then,' Paulina thought, and was glad to think that her time as Lady-in-Waiting was coming to an end.

In the morning, after she had breakfasted with Margarita, a Court-runner brought a letter from the Grand Duke to the *Boudoir*.

The Princess opened the letter, started to read what her fiancé had written with a little smile on her lips, then gave a cry which startled Paulina.

"What is it?" she asked.

"Wonderful, wonderful news!" the Princess replied. "Alexander has a new appointment, and what do you think it is?"

"Tell me," Paulina begged.

"He is to go to Odessa to be Deputy Governor to Prince Voronzov."

Margarita drew in her breath before she said:

"Can you imagine anything more wonderful? We will be away from the Court and St. Petersburg and be able—as Alexander says—to be alone with each other."

Her voice was very moving.

Paulina knew that it was a wise move on the part of the Tsar to send the newly married couple away from all the gossipping, spiteful women of the Court who might make trouble and spoil their happiness.

Prince Voronzov was Viceroy of the new Russian Colony in the far south, and his achievements there had been lauded not only in Russia but all over Europe.

At Odessa he had established commerce, built harbours, Colleges, and hospitals, and gathered round him an aristocratic circle to administer the Province.

He had even introduced steam navigation on the Black Sea and had invited numbers of French viniculturists to supervise the new Crimean vineyards.

Sir Christopher had talked to Paulina quite a lot about what was taking place in the south of Russia. She said now with all sincerity:

"I am sure you will both be very happy there!"

She paused and after a moment added:

"But I feel that it will be . . . unnecessary for me to come with . . . you."

"Of course you must come," the Princess replied.

As she was reading the Grand Duke's letter intently, Paulina felt that her answer was somewhat vague and half-hearted.

Now she walked on, Paulina wondered how she could say tactfully and firmly that she wished to return to Altauss.

But plans were already made and she knew how much the Tsar would resent and oppose any alterations.

The Grand Duke had already gone ahead to St. Petersburg, and tomorrow Margarita would drive beside the Tsar, accompanied by her father, the Grand Duke Louis, to the Cathedral where they would be married.

The Grand Duke's sisters were all to be bridesmaids, besides several other relatives of the Tsar.

Paulina knew it would be a long-drawn-out service while crowns were held over the bride and bridegroom's heads by a relay of attendants.

Then there would be a Reception at the Winter Palace which she was quite sure would be spectacular and unusual.

After this, the newly married couple would drive to a Palace just outside the city, from which they would return two days later to start the long journey south to Odessa.

Paulina felt not only that she was unnecessary as an attendant on the Princess but also that she would be living even farther away from home, and from . . .

She stopped suddenly, knowing her thoughts were too involved for her to carry them any further.

She wanted to run away and hide.

The truth confronted her and she could not escape from it.

Not only was it something of which she was ashamed of feeling, but also to know whom she must leave behind made her feel as if a dagger were piercing her heart.

She stood still beside exquisitely constructed water-gardens, with cascades falling over miniature rocks and crags, and deep pools filled with the exquisite blossoms of water-lilies round whose deep green leaves swam golden fish.

It was all very beautiful but at the same time very artificial, and Paulina had a sudden yearning to be riding in the open country, the wind in her hair and face, the wild flowers peeping through the grass beneath her horse's hooves.

"If only I could ask someone's advice as to what I

should do," she said aloud, and started as she heard footsteps behind her.

She turned her head, expecting to see a gardener or perhaps one of the Court-runners sent to fetch her back to the Palace.

Then she was very still.

Coming through the flowering shrubs, resplendent in his red tunic and looking, she thought, even more handsome than usual, was Prince Maximus.

He moved towards her, and she had no idea how lovely she looked as she stood waiting for him in her simple muslin gown with the blue sash round her waist which echoed the colour of her eyes.

She was silhouetted against a waterfall which fell behind her in a crystal stream from an artificial crag into the stream below.

She felt her heart turn over in her breast and then begin to beat so loudly that she was afraid he might be aware of it.

He reached her side and stood looking at her.

Because she was so shy, she could not meet his eyes.

"I saw you leave the Palace," he said, "and I somehow thought you would find your way here."

"I . . . wanted to . . . think."

"I can understand that. I was afraid you might be perturbed when you heard the Tsar's new plans for Margarita and her husband."

"It is . . . wonderful for . . . them."

She wondered why it was so difficult to speak, and every word she spoke felt as if it must be dragged from between her lips.

"I agree," the Prince said, "but what does it mean to you?"

She had the strange feeling that, without explanation, he understood what she had been thinking and feeling.

Because he obviously expected a reply to his question, she said hesitantly:

"Your . . . family have been so . . . kind to me, but I think I am . . . really . . . unnecessary and I would . . . like to return . . . home."

"Have you suggested this to my sister?"

"I mentioned it when she received a letter from the Grand Duke telling her what had been planned," Paulina responded. "But she was so happy to be going away after being married that she was not really . . . thinking of . . . me."

There was silence and then the Prince said:

"If you go either to Altauss or to Odessa, I shall lose you."

The way he spoke and what he said was so astonishing that Paulina looked at him in bewilderment, thinking that she must be mistaken in what she had just heard.

He was somehow nearer to her than she had expected, and as her eyes met his she was held captive and it was impossible for her to look away.

For what seemed a long, long time they looked at each other, until the Prince said:

"You know what I am feeling, Paulina. What can I say, or what can I do?"

There was a desperate note in his voice which made Paulina instinctively want to hold out her hands towards him. Instead, she could only stand still, trembling.

"I have fought against it," he went on, "but it is greater than I, and although I knew I should not follow you here, you drew me like a magnet and I had not the strength to keep away."

"Please . . . please," Paulina said in a voice he could barely hear. "I understand . . . but you must not say . . . any more."

"Why not?" the Prince asked defiantly. "I am afraid of nothing and nobody, except hurting you."

"You will not hurt me," Paulina said, "but you know we must not . . . see each other again."

Even as she said the words, it was like stabbing herself with a thousand knives.

She could feel the strange vibrations which he evoked in her ever since they had first met becoming stronger, more irresistible, and although he had not moved, she felt as if he had touched her.

The Prince drew in his breath.

"I love you. I have loved you since the first moment I saw you. I could not imagine someone could be so beautiful and at the same time so young, so innocent and untouched."

His voice made Paulina quiver and her eyes fell before his.

She looked down at her clasped hands, her knuckles white from the pressure of her fingers.

"I love you, I love you!" the Prince said. "I swear to you on everything I hold sacred and holy that I have never felt like this about any other woman in my life before."

Because to hear it was so wonderful, Paulina could not stop herself from asking:

"Is that . . . true?"

"I think you know it is true."

He drew in his breath before he continued:

"We have been able to read each other's thoughts because we are so close to each other. We belong, and I know now I have been searching for you all by life."

Paulina wanted to say that he was everything she had dreamt a man would be. Strong, masculine, brave, and at the same time kind, considerate, and understanding.

But the words would not come to her lips and she could only stand, fighting to prevent herself from telling him what he wanted to hear.

After a moment the Prince said almost harshly:

"I shall return to my Regiment. Only by fighting violently and incessantly can I try to forget you."

She gave a little cry as she said:

"You must be . . . careful! Please . . . please be . . . careful . . . for my sake. If anything . . . happened to you . . ."

She looked up at him as she spoke.

A light came into his eyes and her voice died away.

"If anything happened to me?" he repeated slowly. "What would you feel?"

She did not answer, and after a moment he added: "Tell me—I want to know."

She still did not answer, and he took a step nearer to her.

"Tell me," he commanded.

She looked up at him, and it was as if a dam broke within her.

"I . . . would want to . . . die . . . too," she whispered.

"My darling, my sweet."

The Prince put his arms round her and held her close against him. She put her head against his shoulder.

For a moment they just stood there.

Then, as if the words were forced from him:

"I love you, oh, God, how I love you!"

He turned her face up to his and looked down at her as if he would imprint her beauty on his mind forever. Then he pulled her closer and his lips were on hers.

It was a very gentle kiss—the kiss of a man to whom a woman is sacred and whom he approaches with reverence. But as he felt the soft, sweet surrender of Paulina's mouth, his lips grew more insistent, more demanding.

To Paulina it was everything she had dreamt of and longed for.

Every moment since she had come to Russia, her love for the Prince had been growing hour by hour, minute by minute.

Now he awoke in her a rapture of ecstasy that contained all the beauty of the sun and the flowers. It held too the music she heard in the songs of the birds and in the movement of the wind in the trees.

His arms tightened and he drew her closer still.

It seemed to Paulina as if the sun invaded her whole body and ran through her breast to her throat and from her throat to her lips! She knew that she gave the Prince not only her heart but her soul.

He carried her up into the sky and they were no longer human but part of the Divine. It was only when she felt as if the heat of the sun was on his lips that she gave a strangled little cry and turned her face to hide it against his neck.

"My precious, my beautiful little love," the Prince said in a voice that was unsteady. "You must forgive me, but I can no more prevent myself from kissing you prevent myself from breathing. I love you."

Paulina murmured:

"I love . . . you with . . . all my . . . heart."

His arms tightened instinctively, then he said in a voice raw with pain:

"Oh, my God, why did this have to happen to us?"

Because she hated him to suffer, Paulina raised her head to say incoherently:

"You are . . . so . . . wonderful . . . so magnificent . . . we must . . . not have any . . . regrets."

Now as she spoke she knew the breadth and depth and wonder of their love, and that when he left her it would be agony beyond words.

"You are mine," he said, "mine, mine! It was meant by God that we should belong to each other. Yet you know, my darling, that a sword divided us from each other, or rather—a crown."

Paulina gave a deep sigh.

"Yes . . . I know," she whispered. "But I shall always be . . . grateful that you . . . love me, and I know that . . . no man could ever . . . mean to me what you . . . mean now."

"You must not say such things," the Prince said.

"You must go back to Altauss and marry someone kind and suitable, who will worship you as I do."

"Whatever he was . . . like . . . I would have no wish to . . . marry him," Paulina answered. "How could I . . . loving you?"

"My sweet, my precious little flower, you must not think like that. Because you will never see me again when I leave after the wedding, you will forget, of course you will forget."

"And . . . will you . . . forget me . . . too?" Paulina asked.

The pain on the Prince's face was almost agonising.

"I shall try," he answered, "but I know it will be impossible."

He gave a deep sigh.

"What have you done to me? Everywhere I look I will see your face, every voice I hear will be yours. At night I shall lie awake cursing the stars because they remind me of you."

"I will be . . . looking at them . . . too," Paulina said, "and we . . . both know they are . . . out of . . . reach."

"What can I do?" the Prince asked. "What can I do?"

As he spoke, because they were so closely attuned to each other, Paulina knew that he was thinking of Marie-Celeste, the Frenchwoman who had lived for so many years with the Grand Duke.

Almost as if he had asked the question, Paulina said:

"I could not . . . hurt my . . . father."

"Do you really think I would ask such a thing of you?" the Prince enquired angrily. "You are perfect, and I would not spoil anything so beautiful. I have no right to touch you, let alone kiss you."

He paused before he said in a low voice:

"And yet the rapture of that kiss will remain with me all my life. It is the first time a man's lips have ever touched yours, and I would give my right arm to know that it was also the last."

"I do not wish that . . . anyone else should . . . kiss me," Paulina said. "It could . . . never . . . never be as . . . wonderful with . . . anyone else."

"That is what I want you to feel," the Prince said. "Yet it is selfish and cruel of me to try to spoil your life, and I have no excuse. Because I am so much older than you, my beautiful one, I should be able to control myself."

Looking up at the skies, he went on:

"If it had not been for Margarita's marriage, I would have gone away two days ago, or at any rate not have come to Tsarskoe-Selo."

"You must not . . . blame yourself," Paulina said. "I wanted . . . you . . . too."

"Oh, my sweet, I could feel you drawing me to you," the Prince said, "as I always feel the magnetism that exists between us, pulling me to you."

He looked down at her with an expression of despair in his eyes.

"Every inch of the way I travelled here I could feel you calling me, drawing me. You are everything I have desired, looked for, and wished to live for, now and for eternity."

Paulina rested her head against his shoulder and said softly:

"I . . . feel as if we are . . . dreaming."

"If we were dreaming it would be far easier," the Prince said harshly. "We have to go on living—alone— without each other."

She felt his lips on her hair.

"Somehow in my heart I always believed that if a man was fortunate enough he would find the other half of himself. And yet some cynical part of my mind told me it was just a fairy-tale and as far as I was concerned it would never come true."

He kissed her forehead before he continued:

"You are the other half of me. I know now I was aware of it from the very first moment we looked at each other. You have everything I want in a woman—sensitivity, sweetness, compassion, loyalty, and above all a beauty which tears at my very heart."

"I thought you would never . . . notice me while Princess . . . Natasha was . . . there," Paulina said.

The Prince gave a little laugh which had no humour in it.

"There are always 'Natashas' in every man's life," he answered. "They are the temptations of St. Anthony, to drown the senses with everything that is physical and material."

He put his fingers under Paulina's chin and turned her face up to his. His face altered as he said gently:

"You, my darling, arouse the spiritual side of a man. You inspire me to raise my eyes to the stars, to climb the mountains from which one can see new horizons and beyond them Paradise."

He spoke so seriously that Paulina felt that he roused in her something so sacred and so beautiful it was almost as if she were receiving a sacrament in Church.

"This is . . . what I have . . . prayed I might give the . . . man I . . . loved," she said.

"It is what you have given me," the Prince answered, "which is why my darling, I am now going to leave you, and we must not be together again before the wedding. That will be the last time we shall see each other."

He spoke with a sound of infinite sadness in his voice.

Paulina gave a little cry.

"I cannot . . . bear it!" she protested. "I am not . . . strong like . . . you. I want to be with you . . . to see you . . . to hear your voice . . . and to . . . love you."

The Prince groaned and it was an expression of pain. Then he laid his cheek against hers and said:

"I shall think of you, dream of you, and wherever I am, I shall feel somehow that you are near me. I shall never really lose you because you and I are indivisible."

"I shall . . . feel that . . . too," Paulina replied. "Yet, however much my prayers reach out towards you . . . I shall be alone and . . . lonely because you . . . are not . . . with me."

"I shall be the same," the Prince said. "But because we have met, because I have found you and you have given me your love, I shall not be the same man I was before, but a very much better one."

"You are fine, noble, and everything I want you to be," Paulina cried. "However long we may be . . . parted in this life . . . I somehow feel . . . one day perhaps in a . . . thousand years' time . . . we shall be . . . together."

The Prince did not answer and she felt as if his suffering was past words.

Instead he held her very closely against him for what seemed a long time. Then once again he looked down into her face.

"You are mine," he said very quietly, "'til the stars fall from the sky and the waters of the sea are dry."

Then his lips came down on hers.

Although he held her captive, his kiss was different from the one he had given her before, and Paulina had the strange feeling that he had already left her.

It was a kiss without passion, a kiss of reverence, a kiss which irrevocably united them so that they would never be divided from each other.

She reverberated to the wonder of it and felt the sunshine pass through her body and from her lips to his.

It was so marvellous, so glorious, that once again he was carrying her up into the sky.

Suddenly he took his arms from her, and before she could speak—or even beg him not to go—he had moved away, disappearing through the thick shrubs.

She stood trembling, unable to believe he had really gone, and wanting to call him back, but her voice died in her throat.

Then as the full impact of what had happened to

her made itself felt, she sank very slowly down on the grass beside the stream and hid her face in her hands.

The rapture he had aroused in her body battled with her mind and forced her to face the truth—that everything was over.

When at last she acknowledged that there was no hope and, although she might see him again in the distance, they were parted forever, the tears came.

Slowly, agonisingly, they crept down her cheeks and she felt as if each one were a drop of blood from her heart.

*   *   *

It was a long time before Paulina walked back slowly, as if she had suddenly grown very old, towards the Palace.

She entered by a side door and, with her head bent, walked along the passages.

For the first time since she had come to Tsarskoe-Selo she took no notice of the exquisite paintings which had been collected by Catherine the Great from all over Europe.

She did not see the inlaid furniture or the carpets and rugs from Persia and Samarkand.

Instead, Paulina felt as if she had walked into a thick fog in which there was no light but only the darkness of despair, and she was controlled by custom and convention rather than by any choice of her own will.

She walked up the stairs and as she reached the landing she could hear voices and laughter coming from the Princess's bedroom, and she guessed that the Grand Duke's sisters were with her and they had not noticed her absence.

She went into her bedroom and saw that while she had been away the maids had packed her large leather trunk. It was ready to follow her to St. Petersburg tomorrow, moving either before or after the bridal procession had left the Palace.

The only things that remained unpacked were the gown that Paulina was to wear at dinner this evening and the one she had chosen for the wedding.

It was simple compared with the very elaborate *toilettes* of the Tsarina and the other ladies. Of sky-blue silk, it was the same tone of blue as her eyes.

She knew it was very becoming, and as it flashed through her mind that the Prince would admire her, she knew that was something she should no longer think about.

Then the agony of knowing that after tomorrow she would never see him again was so intense that she felt as if her legs would no longer carry her, and she sat down beside her bed.

After the ceremony in the Cathedral she would follow Margarita and the Grand Duke to the Palace where they were staying for the first night of the honeymoon.

Prince Maximus, however, would set off for the Caucasus to renew the dangerous campaign in which already so many Russians had been killed.

"How can I . . . bear it?" Paulina asked herself, knowing at the same time that there was no alternative.

"I must go . . . home," she told herself.

She went to the desk to start writing a letter to her father, begging him to ask for her return.

She knew even as she began to write that it would be a very long time before she would receive his reply, and she wondered how she could bear to remain patiently in Odessa, waiting and waiting until she heard from him.

She tried to plan some means of going home immediately, to think of excuses that would prevent her from accompanying the bride and bridegroom to the south.

It was a long journey home, however, whether she

went by sea or by land, and she would be afraid to undertake it alone.

"Alone . . . alone," the words seemed to haunt her.

She was alone, utterly and completely alone, without Prince Maximus.

However many people were round her, she would find herself isolated and bereft because he had taken her heart and soul with him, and as love was a stronger emotion than any other, in the future she would be nothing but an empty shell.

She would live and breathe, smile and talk, ride and dance; but although she might appear to be a living and breathing person, she would really be nothing but a ghost, and her real self would be with the man she loved.

"This was the true love I wanted and prayed for," she said aloud. "Yet now it is crucifying me."

* * *

Later, because it was expected of her, Paulina washed her face and forced herself to join the Princess in her *Boudoir.*

Margarita, wearing a very attractive and becoming negligé which was part of her trousseau, was lying on a chaise-longue, while seated round her were the Grand Duke's sisters, opening the presents that had just arrived by messenger from St. Petersburg.

"Another gold comfit dish," one of them exclaimed as Paulina entered the room. "You will be able to pave a terrace with them if you have any more!"

Everyone laughed. Then the Princess looked up and saw Paulina in the doorway.

"I wondered what had happened to you, dearest Paulina!" she exclaimed. "Come and look at the jewellery I have received. The Tsarina has given me a string of pearls that will reach from my neck to my knees."

It was certainly very impressive. At the same time, Paulina thought it was too large and too opulent to be

really becoming to anyone as slim and with such deli-
cate features as Margarita.

There were a great many other things to see and
admire. Paulina was quiet, finding it difficult to concentrate on what was being said.

No-one noticed.

Only when it was time to change for the early
dinner that the Tsar insisted upon did Paulina question
whether Prince Maximus would be present. She wondered
if she could bear to watch him across the table without
revealing her feelings.

However, when she and the Princess arrived downstairs there was no sign of Prince Maximus, and the
dinner-party was small, since some of the elderly relatives had already left for St. Petersburg.

The Tsar was in a good temper, talking incessantly
about the service for which he had not only arranged
the time and the place but had also chosen the Priests,
the prayers, and even the music.

It was so typical of him, Paulina knew, to have such
an eye for detail. When she said so in polite terms to an
elderly Statesman who was sitting next to her, he
laughed and said:

"Only the Tsar could manage to interfere with
details in every branch of life in this enormous country.
In St. Petersburg, if the fire-bell rings, he runs out and
tells the firemen what to do."

Paulina laughed because it was expected of her. At
the same time, she felt that if the Tsar overheard the
conversation, he might consider it an insult.

After dinner the ladies talked for a little while with
the Tsarina until she said to Margarita:

"I think, dearest child, you should retire early and
get as much beauty-sleep as you can. Tomorrow will be
not only a long day but an exciting one. I want you to
look very beautiful for our beloved Alexander."

"I certainly hope, Ma'am, that he will think I am
beautiful," the Princess replied.

The Tsarina said with affection:

"You will be the loveliest bride Russia has seen for a long time. And I know you will be thrilled by what has been arranged for you in St. Petersburg."

"Do tell me what it is!" Margarita cried.

The Tsarina shook her head.

"It is to be a surprise, so the Tsar likes to keep it a secret until the very last moment."

"That is true," said the Tsar, who had overheard the conversation. "I want your wedding-day to be something you will remember all your life."

"I am sure I shall do that, Sire," Margarita replied.

She bade everyone good-night, and although it was only a few minutes after eight o'clock, she and Paulina went upstairs.

While her maid undressed her, Margarita talked excitedly about the wedding and kept saying over and over again how happy she was.

When finally they were alone she said:

"How can I have been so foolish as to think I was making a mistake by coming to live in Russia? It is a perfect place, a Heaven upon earth! I know that when I am Alexander's wife I shall feel as if we have both been transported into Paradise."

"I am sure you will," Paulina said, trying not to reflect that she would feel the same if she were marrying Prince Maximus.

As if there was something in her voice which told the Princess that something was wrong, she said quickly:

"Once we get to Odessa, dearest, and I have a moment to myself, I am going to concentrate on finding you a husband as charming, handsome, and adorable as Alexander! But of course, I doubt if another man like him exists."

She laughed, then added:

"I shall find you someone nearly as nice because I am so happy and I want everyone to be happy too."

Paulina did not say that there was only one man

who could make her happy and it was a waste of time for the Princess to try to marry her off to somebody else.

Instead, she just smiled and made an appropriate reply. Finally, after talking to the Princess until nearly ten o'clock, she kissed her good-night and went to her own room.

The maid helped her out of her thin gown and packed it on top of the trunk.

When she had put on her nightgown, instead of getting into bed Paulina thought she would finish her letter to her father.

She had somehow to make him understand that she must come home.

'At home I will not have to pretend,' Paulina thought. 'If I feel unhappy, I can be unhappy without anyone questioning it or being curious about me.'

She went to the elegant French writing-desk which stood in the window and started to write swiftly in her elegant, well-formed writing.

She was too wise to put in anything that could be understood by the spies, who she was certain censored every letter that went from the Palace before it was despatched.

She said merely that she was very homesick and, for reasons that she would tell him when she saw him, she wanted to come home.

She was sure her father would read between the lines and think perhaps she was having difficulty in keeping some ardent Russian at arm's-length.

However, what he thought did not matter as long as Sir Christopher brought diplomatic pressure to have his daughter home with him.

"*I love you, and only you would understand that I should come back immediately,*" Paulina wrote, then she underlined the last word.

She then signed her name and put the letter in an envelope.

She addressed it to her father at the Legion in Windenstadt and decided it would be quicker to take it with her to St. Petersburg rather than send it from here.

If she gave it to a Court-runner at the Winter Palace to take to the British Embassy, it would be sent in the Diplomatic Bag without being read.

For a moment she hesitated, wondering if she should be more explicit, then decided it would be a mistake to take any chance.

For the Tsar to become aware of what was happening would be disastrous. She was quite sure his reaction would be a very unpleasant one.

'I will send it as it is,' she thought, and put it ready beside the bag and gloves she was to take with her on the drive tomorrow morning.

She was just about to take off her negligé and get into bed when she thought she would have a last look from the window at the garden.

She would never come to Tsarskoe-Selo again, yet she would always remember that it was here that Prince Maximus had told her of his love and kissed her.

Even to think of his lips on hers made the ecstasy he had aroused in her flow again through her body.

She felt again as if a streak of sunshine shot through her breasts and up into her lips.

It was so rapturous, so wonderful, that once again she was quivering as she had when the Prince touched her.

She shut her eyes so that for a moment she could almost imagine she was in his arms. She was his as he had said she was.

"I love . . . you . . . I love you."

Then as she whispered the words she heard a strange little click behind her, and turning her head she was frozen into immobility.

Coming through a secret door in the panelling was the Prince.

Chapter Six

After the Prince left Paulina, he had walked back to the Palace, where he ordered a horse to be brought from the stables.

While he was waiting for it, he told one of the *Aides-de-Camp* to inform the Tsar that he had gone riding and regretted that he might not be back in time for dinner and hoped His Imperial Majesty would excuse him from being present.

When the horse arrived it was a spirited animal which was still not completely broken in, and the Prince rode off, determined to try to ease the tumult in his mind and heart by violent exercise.

He rode until his mount was sweating and he himself felt breathless.

However, when he was obliged to conform to a more ordinary pace, his thoughts and feelings swept over him like a flood-tide.

How could he have imagined, he asked himself, that he would ever fall in love as he had now, in a manner which was not only irrevocable and overwhelming but was something that would never happen again.

There had been many women in the Prince's life, and he had been attracted, fascinated, and even infatuated with them.

The majority had been like Princess Natasha, who had evoked in him a fiery response which he knew in a secret part of his mind was not a love that endured nor what unconsciously he was striving to find.

He had never analysed exactly what he wanted.

But because he was both sensitive and idealistic, there was somewhere, hidden in the deepest reserves of his character, a shrine in which he had erected the image of the ideal woman to whom he would give not only his heart but his soul.

Instinctively he had been aware that like the Holy Grail it was what he sought but which, as the years passed, he cynically thought he would never find.

Then when he had seen Paulina for the first time, it was as if she were enveloped with a celestial light!

He felt her vibrations reaching out towards him and he knew instinctively, positively, that it was she whom he had sought.

He rode on, seeing nothing of the lovely countryside, the trees heavy with blossoms, the grass thick with flowers.

Instead, he could see only the rapture of Paulina's face when he had kissed her and felt the soft sweetness of her lips, which had brought him an ecstasy which he had never known before.

Everything that other women had taught him, everything they aroused in him, was, he knew now, a very pale and insubstantial shadow of real love.

Having found Paulina and knowing that the love he had for her and she for him was a gift of God, there was nothing he could do except blot her out of his life and try to forget.

Had she not been so perfect in her purity, he knew that he might, in other circumstances, have tried to seduce her.

Yet, as things were between them, to do so would be an offence against God, against everything he held sacred, against the very faith in which he believed.

"I love her," he told the sky above him, "and I

must be big enough to pray for her happiness without me."

However, he knew that in the future he would never find the happiness he sought.

While Paulina's face would haunt him, the memory of her lips and of her body held close against his would prevent him from desiring any other woman in the way he had in the past.

It was growing late when he turned back towards the Palace.

The Prince felt as if he had lived through a century of time and in the passing of a few hours had become very much older.

There was nothing he could do.

Fate had given him a glimpse of Heaven, only to slam the gates of it in his face and leave him outside with no chance of ever entering it again.

By the time the Prince reached the Palace, he was tired and so was his horse.

He handed the animal over to a groom and stepped in through a front door.

As he did so, as servant came hurrying towards him to say:

"His Imperial Majesty wished to speak to Your Royal Highness."

"Now?" the Prince queried.

"Immediately Your Royal Highness returned."

The Prince glanced at the huge clock in the Hall, made of green malachite with the figures of the hours outlined in precious stones.

He knew that by this time dinner would be over, the ladies would have withdrawn to rest, and the gentlemen would be alone at their ease.

"Where is His Majesty?"

"In his study, Your Royal Highness."

The servant walked ahead to lead the way.

The Prince followed with a sigh, knowing the last

thing he wanted at the moment was a confidential talk with the Tsar.

He would have liked to wash and change before such an audience, but he knew that if the Tsar requested his presence immediately on his return, it was an order that he was required to obey.

With his spurs clanking, he walked down numerous passages before the door of the Tsar's Study was opened.

"His Royal Highness Prince Maximus of Altauss, Your Imperial Majesty."

The Tsar, sitting at his desk with a large pile of papers in front of him, looked up with a smile.

"You have returned, Maximus," he said. "What was the need for such lengthy exercise?"

"I am used to being in the saddle in the Caucasus, Sire," the Prince replied. "I must not get out of practice before I return."

As he spoke he thought that he would tell the Tsar now that he intended to return to his Regiment immediately after Margarita was married.

Before he could speak, the Tsar said:

"Sit down, Maximus. I want to talk to you."

The Prince obeyed, choosing a rather hard, uncomfortable chair on the other side of the desk.

The Tsar looked down at the papers in front of him and there was a little pause before he said:

"I have in front of me a report, speaking in most glowing terms of your bravery, your leadership, and the part you have played in bringing nearer the defeat of Shamyl."

The Prince inclined his head in acknowledgement, and the Tsar, not waiting for him to speak, went on:

"There are obviously other awards you must have in the future besides the Order of St. George, with which you have recently been decorated. I also have a personal award of my own to give you."

"You are very gracious, Sire," the Prince murmured.

He could not help feeling how little such praise counted at this moment when a month ago he would have been elated by it.

Now he felt only as if his body were cold and empty, and he knew that his longing for Paulina was preventing him from feeling any other emotion apart from the agony of losing her.

"What I have to suggest," the Tsar was saying, "is something that will not only please you, Maximus, but will also delight your father."

Again the Tsar paused, but this time as if for dramatic effect, before he said:

"I have decided to welcome you as a close member of my family, and you will marry my niece, the Grand Duchess Catherine."

If the Tsar had fired his pistol at the Prince, or dropped a cannon-ball at his feet, the surprise could not have been more explosive.

For a moment the Prince felt he could not have understood correctly what the Tsar said.

As he stared across the desk at him, His Imperial Majesty chuckled.

"That has surprised you?" he questioned. "I thought it would. I have grown fond of you. I only wish my other relatives had your courage and ingenuity."

Speechless, the Prince could find no words to reply, and the Tsar continued:

"Catherine will make you a good wife, and it means that the Tsarina and I will see more of you. We will plan your marriage tomorrow after your sister's wedding is over, and it should not be long delayed."

As he finished speaking the Tsar rose to his feet in his usual abrupt manner and the interview was at an end.

Feeling as if he were sleep-walking, the Prince managed to get to his feet.

"It is—difficult to know—what to say, Sire," he murmured.

But the Tsar's over-active mind had already disposed of one problem and was ready for the next. He was not listening to the Prince but was ringing the gold bell which lay on his desk.

Immediately the door opened.

"Send in Count Benckendorff," he ordered.

As the Prince bowed his way to the door, Count Benckendorff of the Third Section came in.

When Prince Maximus walked away from the Tsar's Study along the passages and corridors to his own room, he felt as if he had been struck on the head with a heavy instrument.

As his valet removed his boots and helped him take off his clothes before bathing, he realised that he was caught in a trap from which there was no escape.

As an officer in the Imperial Russian Army, he must obey the Tsar even though he himself was of another nationality.

Gradually the numbness which made him feel as if his brain ceased to function began to pass.

He became aware actively and positively that while every instinct in his body yearned for Paulina, he had no wish to marry the Grand Duchess Catherine.

Also, he had no desire to be little more than a serf to a tyrannical and absolute Monarch.

The Prince had been in many dangerously tight corners in his life.

In the Caucasus they said he had a charmed existence comparable only to that of Shamyl himself, who was noted for having a supernatural ability to escape from the most impossible situations.

"I will not do it," the Prince said aloud.

He knew as he spoke the words that there would be no greater hell than to lose not only the woman he loved but also every vestige of independence.

In his bedroom his valet had laid out his evening-clothes, expecting him as usual to join the other members of the party downstairs.

The Prince waved them away and put on a fresh edition of his uniform, noting grimly the decorations on his left breast.

"Everything else is packed, Your Royal Highness," the valet said as the Prince buttoned the front of his tunic.

"Everything?" the Prince queried.

"Except the full-dress uniform that Your Royal Highness will wear at the wedding."

"Put them in the trunk," the Prince commented. "I may leave for St. Petersburg this evening."

"Very good, Your Highness."

The Prince hesitated for a moment, then said:

"Wait here for me, I shall have further orders for you."

As he spoke he went from the room, shutting the door behind him.

*   *   *

Paulina stared at the Prince incredulously.

"Why are ... you here ... what do ... you want?"

There was a frightened note in her voice which swept from her eyes the rapture which had been there at the first sight of him.

The Prince pushed back into place the secret panel through which he had entered her room, and as he came slowly towards her with his eyes on her face, he said:

"Forgive me, my darling, for startling you. I have to ask you a question which is more important to me than anything else in the world."

"Now ... at this ... moment?" Paulina faltered.

She glanced over her shoulder as she spoke, fearing that what they were saying would be overheard by someone listening.

She was also bewildered that the Prince had come to her through a secret entrance.

"There is no time to lose," the Prince said. "And I

think, for the moment anyway, anything we say to each
other will be private."

He was speaking in English.

Before Paulina could reply, he moved a step nearer
still.

She waited apprehensively, still bemused by his
sudden appearance, feeling it was wrong that he should
be there.

At the same time, she was unable to prevent the
rapture from rising within her because she was seeing
him again and he was close to her.

The Prince drew in his breath, then he said, his
voice very deep and low:

"Will you marry me, Paulina?"

She stared at him as if she did not understand what
he had said.

"M-marry...you?" she stammered almost inaudibly.

The Prince put his hands out and took hers.

She felt herself tremble because he was touching
her. At the same time, she was trying to realise what he
had asked.

"I love you," the Prince said, "and I think you love
me. I have to ask whether you are prepared, for the
sake of our love, to go into exile and in doing so risk
danger and even perhaps death."

Paulina's fingers tightened on his.

"I do...not...understand."

"Why should you?" the Prince asked. "But I will
try to explain, my precious love. I would not ask this of
you if I did not believe that whatever such an action
may entail, I can make you happy."

He waited for her answer, and, raising her eyes to
his, Paulina said:

"I love...you and I...want to do...anything
you...wish. But how is it...possible for...us to
be...married?"

"You were meant to be my wife," the Prince
answered. "That you are mine is written in the stars. We

were created for each other, my precious, and we belong to each other. But we have to take risks that may frighten you."

"I would . . . risk . . . anything to be your . . . wife," Paulina said simply.

As she spoke she saw the Prince's eyes light as if the stars were reflected in them, and he bent his head.

His lips were on her hand, kissing first the back of it and then turning it over to press his mouth possessively and demandingly against the palm.

"I worship you," he said quietly.

Then, almost as if he called himself to attention, he took his hand from hers and said:

"The Tsar has just informed me that I am to marry his niece, the Grand Duchess Catherine."

Paulina's lips parted to give a cry, but it was stifled in her throat, and before she could make a sound the Prince went on:

"I knew then, as I knew before, that no woman could take your place in my life, but also that I would fight to possess you or die in the attempt."

"H-how . . . could you . . . r-risk your l-life for . . . me?" Paulina stammered.

"I would risk a hundred lives if I had them," the Prince answered. "I know now I was being a coward in running away from something so tremendous, so important, that I must win or die if I cannot be victorious."

"No . . . no!" Paulina cried.

"I am talking about you, my darling," the Prince said, "and I was idiotic to think that I could leave you or live without you."

"How . . . can we be . . . together?" she whispered.

"That is what I am going to tell you," the Prince answered. "We leave here tonight, immediately."

Paulina stared at him as she asked:

"Can we . . . do . . . that?"

"I will arrange everything," he said. "If you are willing to come with me, then I swear that I shall win the only battle I have ever fought that is worthwhile, and you will be my wife."

Because she could not help herself, Paulina took a step nearer to him and put out her hands.

She felt herself already being carried away by the elation and determination in the Prince's voice.

Too, she felt his vibrations drawing her and holding her so that she was already part of him.

As if he understood, he put his arm round her and held her against him. Then looked down at her and continued quietly:

"We will leave here in a *drosky* which will carry us to St. Petersburg. There we will take a train which will carry us across Russia, through Poland, and into Altauss."

"Will they not . . . not stop . . . us?" Paulina questioned.

"We shall have a long start."

"But when . . . they learn that . . . we have gone?"

"They will try."

As they spoke, they both knew that "they" meant the Tsar and were well aware that there was nothing that His Imperial Majesty would resent more than his plans being thwarted, his orders disobeyed.

Paulina suddenly realised that not only was the Prince refusing to marry the Tsar's niece, he was also resigning from the Imperial Russian Army.

"You must . . . not do this . . . you cannot!" she exclaimed. "If His Imperial Majesty wished to accuse you of . . . desertion, you could be . . . shot."

"I am well aware of that," the Prince said, "and that is why , my darling, we have to be clever."

"I cannot let you . . . do this for . . . me," Paulina protested.

"I love you, and that is all that matters."

"Besides," Paulina said in a very small voice, "as I am not Royal, our marriage will not be . . . accepted in . . . Altauss."

The Prince's arm tightened round her.

"I have thought of that. You are wise enough to realise that we must be married as an ordinary man and woman without involving my rank."

"I think," Paulina said, "that it would be a . . . morganatic . . . marriage."

"It will," the Prince agreed, "and the only person who could dissolve a morganatic marriage would be my father. If he does so, I shall renounce my rights as his heir."

For a moment Paulina felt she could not have heard him correctly. Then she gave a cry which came from the very depths of her being.

"No . . . no . . . I could not ask that of you! It is wrong! You mean so . . . much to the people in . . . Altauss!"

"You mean so much to me," the Prince replied. "If Altauss will not accept me as their Ruler, then I will be an ordinary citizen, and I will be perfectly content to be so as long as you are my wife."

"Can you . . . really make . . . such a . . . sacrifice for me?" Paulina asked wonderingly.

"It will not be a sacrifice," the Prince said. "We shall be together, and whatever happens, I swear to you, I shall be truly content and have no regrets."

"But how can you be . . . sure of . . . that?"

With his arms round Paulina, he drew her to the window.

The sun had sunk. Now there was only a translucent glow in the sky where it had been. Overhead, the great sable arc of the Heavens was glittering with stars.

He looked up as he said:

"I said you were a star and, like a star, out of reach. But now you are in my arms. Would it be a sacrifice for a man who could hold a celestial body in his arms and know it was his?"

"It sounds . . . wonderful the way you . . . say it," Paulina whispered. "But suppose when we have been married a little while you grow . . . tired of me? Suppose

you miss the . . . glory of the Russian Army, the pomp
. . . luxury . . . the ceremony . . . we have seen . . . here?"

For an answer, the Prince put his hand under her
chin and tipped her face up to his.

"We will lead a full and varied life, my precious
love," he answered. "I have, as you know, won decorations in the Army and been fêted in the Tsar's Court.
None of it—I swear to you—is of any importance beside
what I feel for you."

"How can you be . . . sure?"

"I am sure! I know it positively, absolutely, in my
mind and also in my soul."

He hesitated for a moment before he went on:

"Our love is greater than any glory a man can
achieve in other fields. Our love is a part of God and is
something which cannot be denied."

The way he spoke was so moving that Paulina felt
the tears come into her eyes. Then she said in a broken
little voice:

"I do not . . . believe any other man could . . . anything
so wonderful! But I know I should . . . think of . . . you
and . . . refuse to allow you to do . . . anything so . . . drastic
just for . . . me."

The Prince smiled.

"It is not a question whether you will allow it or
not allow it. Because you said you loved me, it is
something I intend to do. The only thing that frightens
me is that I am risking your good name and perhaps
your very life in doing what I know is right for us both."

"I am not . . . afraid," Paulina answered.

It was then that he kissed her. His lips touched
hers, at first gently and then more insistently.

Almost before she could feel the rapture rising
within her, the sunshine moving through her body
towards her lips, he said:

"If you will come with me, we must leave at once."

"Supposing they stop . . . us?" Paulina asked.

"Leave everything to me," he said. "Get dressed. I see your trunk is ready. I will send a servant for it."

She felt that he was about to leave and held on to him with both hands.

"You are sure . . . quite sure . . . you should do this?" she asked. "Remember, you are a Prince and I am only a . . . commoner."

"Remember only that I love you," the Prince replied, "and you said you loved me."

He looked at her for a moment, then he went down on one knee, taking her hand in his.

"I swear to you," he said solemnly, "if you will come with me, if you will marry me, not as a Prince but as a man, I will love you, serve you, and make you happy not only for this life but for all eternity."

As if he cemented the vow he made to her, his lips were on her hand, while the tears ran down Paulina's cheeks because there were no words in which to tell him how much she loved him.

*   *   *

Afterwards, Paulina found it hard to remember the frightening moments when they crept down the unfrequented passages and corridors of the Palace and out through a side-door.

She had dressed herself as quickly as she could in the elegant gown and bonnet which had been left out for her journey the following day to St. Petersburg.

She was tying the ribbons under her chin when there was a very faint knock on her door. When she opened it, she saw the Prince's servant.

He did not speak but merely went to her trunk on which Paulina had laid the negligé and nightgown she had been wearing. He fastened and strapped it and, still in silence, carried it from the room.

Paulina waited and then on an impulse went to the desk and wrote a few lines to Margarita.

*"I have gone ahead, Ma'am, to St. Petersburg.
I wish you every possible happiness and blessing on
your Wedding Day and hope that you will find true
love with the Grand Duke. I love you, Ma'am, as I
always have and always will."*

Paulina.

As she finished writing, the Prince came in through
the secret panel and she held out the letter to him.

He read it quickly, then nodded and said:

"That is sensible. It was something I was going to
suggest to you. I have written almost the same thing to
the Tsar. We even think alike."

For a moment it was difficult for Paulina to remember that she must fold the letter and address it to
the Princess.

She left it on the writing-table, and then the
Prince took her by the hand and drew her through the
secret panel.

It was fascinating to see that there was an aperture
between the walls which was large enough to hold a spy
listening to everything that was said in the rooms on
either side.

They stepped out into the next bedroom, which
was empty, and then with the Prince holding her hand
they moved by an intricate route through the Palace so
that they would not be seen.

Only when they were outside and had walked a
little way to where a *drosky* was waiting for them did
the Prince say:

"Now we start the great adventure, my darling,
and I do not want you to be afraid."

Paulina smiled at him. There was no need to say
that she was unafraid; she was only excited at what was
happening.

The Prince's servant had strapped their trunks to
the *drosky*. There were three horses to draw it, and
when they had seated themselves with a rug over their

knees, they set off at a tremendous pace by the light of
the moon, which was just rising in the sky.

Paulina could hardly believe that they had really
left behind the Palace, the Tsar and the Tsarina, the
Grand Duke Louis, Margarita, and the Court officials
who were travelling with them in procession on the
morrow.

As if he felt her thoughts, the Prince said:

"Everyone will think we have gone ahead as so
many people have done, to be at the wedding when the
procession arrives. That gives us time to be well away
from St. Petersburg before any questions are asked
about our absence."

Paulina did not reply because the wind was in her
face and it was difficult to speak, owing to the speed
with which they were travelling.

Instead, she squeezed the Prince's fingers as he
was holding hers under the rug, and he turned his face
to smile at her.

She knew that he understood and that there was
no need for words between them. Their minds were
linked and she was content to leave everything to him.

They reached St. Petersburg in what Paulina thought
must be record time.

When they reached the railway station, which was
only just being built to accommodate the new trains
which were a wonder and an excitement to the Russians,
the Prince was received ceremoniously by a number of
railway officials.

He spoke with authority, and Paulina realised,
because she could now understand Russian, that the
officials believed he had a special mission to undertake
upon behalf of the Tsar.

They were escorted to a coach that was attached to
the ordinary train, and she saw that it was much more
comfortable than she had expected.

Only when they left, after a great deal of saluting
and bowing, was the Prince able to explain:

"We are lucky. This coach had brought some minor German Princeling to the Capital for the wedding, and I have managed to commandeer it for our journey."

"Is that a wise thing to do?" Paulina queried.

The Prince smiled.

"I may as well be hung for a sheep as a lamb."

He was speaking in English, and Paulina replied in a choked voice:

"I am still afraid that . . . somehow the Tsar will manage to . . . stop us."

The train was already moving out of the station and gathering speed, but they were still within the confines of St. Petersburg.

Paulina looked at the houses, the Palaces, the spires and domes they were passing, and had a terrified feeling that at the last moment the Tsar would have learnt of their departure.

The train would come to a halt, and the spies and officials of the Third Section would take them into custody.

While she sat trembling and apprehensive, the Prince was unfastening his sword, obviously ready to make himself comfortable.

"Stop being frightened, my darling," he said as he saw the expression on her face. "So far, so good! I am convinced that by now His Imperial Majesty and the odious Count Benckendorff are sleeping the sleep of the just and will not be the least suspicious that anything untoward has happened until after the wedding has taken place."

"How can you be so . . . sure?" Paulina asked.

"I am sure because love is greater than the pettyfogging plots of men," the Prince replied.

The train was now going a little faster and Paulina felt she must sit down.

The Prince drew her to his side and began to undo the ribbons on her bonnet. He took it off and threw it carelessly down on another seat before he said:

"How can you be so beautiful, and how can I be so lucky as to have found you?"

"I am afraid I have brought you nothing but . . . trouble," Paulina answered. "I also think I am . . . dreaming."

As she spoke she looked out the window and saw that they had already left the city.

Now the moonlight was turning the trees to silver. The houses were getting fewer and soon they would be in the open country.

"It is very late," the Prince said, "and so, my precious, I am going to send you to bed. Try to sleep, because we have a very long journey and we can only pray that even the fastest *drosky* or Cavalry division will be unable to intercept us."

Paulina shivered.

"Can they do . . . that?"

"Only if they can fly as fast as birds, or if the Tsar had a telegraph communication with the stations that lie ahead of us, but it has not yet been introduced in Russia."

"I hope you are right," Paulina said apprehensively.

"So do I," the Prince said. "I refuse to spend two days and nights sitting tense and terrified, when I might be telling you how much I love you and kissing the softness of your lips."

He kissed her as he spoke, and Paulina thought that if they had to die at the end of the journey then it would have been worth the rapture of being in the Prince's arms and knowing his love.

She wanted him to kiss her and go on kissing her.

He pulled her to her feet and they moved unsteadily to the end of the coach, which was separated from where they had been sitting by a curtain.

The Prince pulled it aside and Paulina saw that there was a bedroom fitted out with a bed, a wash-basin, and even a sort of dressing-table at which she could arrange her hair.

"We are very fortunate," the Prince told her. "I anticipated that we would be uncomfortable in an ordinary carriage. This is very much *de luxe*."

"I only hope its owner won't mind us borrowing it," Paulina replied.

"If I know anything of the railway officials, they are like all the other officials in Russia. They have taken quite a large sum of money from me to hire it, the money will go into their own pockets, and the Royal owner will have no idea that it has not sat waiting for him in a siding."

"We can hardly complain," Paulina replied, and the Prince laughed.

As they stood, holding on to the end of the bed as the fast train was swaying, Paulina realised that there was only one bed in the carriage and looked at the Prince with a question in her eyes.

Once again, he knew exactly what she was thinking.

"I love you, my darling," he said, "but I also revere and worship you. I want nothing more than to hold you close and make you mine, but that will wait until you are my wife."

Paulina gave a little sigh and put her head against his shoulder.

"I will never," the Prince went on, "never do anything which I know you would dislike or which would upset you. What I want for you in our life, my beloved, is what you are in yourself, perfection."

He kissed her, then he said:

"Undress and get into bed. I promise you I am going to sleep very comfortably elsewhere in the coach."

"But you want pillows and blankets."

The Prince kissed her cheek.

"I adore you for being so practical," he replied, "but I promise you all those things are provided. The Prussian who owns this coach filled it to capacity with his attendants, and they would have made themselves just as comfortable as I intend to be."

He pulled her closer and kissed her again—this time with demanding passion which left her breathless.

Then the heavy curtain fell behind him and she was alone.

Paulina undressed quickly. She got into the bed and found it surprisingly comfortable.

Tired though she was, she was very conscious that the Prince was very near and she was setting off on a wild adventure which might have terrible repercussions and would certainly upset and perhaps infuriate the Prince's father, the Grand Duke Louis.

She felt that her own father would understand; after all, he had wanted her to find love, and that was what she had found. But whether he would approve of the way the Prince had taken the law into his own hands she was not certain.

'At least it will be a very exciting story to tell our children and our grandchildren,' she thought.

Then as she cuddled down against the soft pillows, she blushed at the idea and was glad that at the moment the Prince could not hear her.

Chapter Seven

"Tomorrow, with God's help," the Prince said, "we will cross the frontier."

For a moment Paulina did not reply.

She was thinking that she had never been so happy in her life as the train rattled over the ocean-flat plains of western Russia and the barren land of Poland.

To be with the Prince, to talk to him, to listen to his words of love, was like being transported into Paradise, and she could not bear that it should come to an end.

"I wish we could . . . stay here . . . forever," she murmured at length.

The Prince put his arms consolingly round her, and at the same time he was smiling.

"I think you would find it a somewhat restrictive life."

"I would be with . . . you and we would be . . . alone."

His eyes were very tender as he said:

"Do you suppose it has not been wonderful for me too? But I want more, my precious—I want you to be my wife."

"That is . . . what I . . . want," Paulina replied, "but I am . . . afraid."

Every time the train stopped to refuel with wood, which it burnt so quickly, they had to wait a long time at some primitive wayside station.

Despite her happiness, Paulina was afraid when

they stopped that this would be the opportunity for the Tsar's guards, who she was certain were following them, to take them captive.

Only when the wood was piled high in the engine tender again and the engine, puffing and blowing out clouds of smoke, chugged slowly on its way could she give a deep sigh of relief.

As they went, the Prince had explained to her that the train went straight to Prussia, and once they had crossed the border they would have to obtain a carriage and horses to drive them on to Altauss.

"Then we shall be . . . safe?" Paulina asked.

"His Imperial Majesty has no jurisdiction in Prussia," the Prince replied, "or, thank Heaven, in my own country."

Paulina looked at him swiftly.

She knew only too well how much Altauss meant to him and that if he abdicated as he had threatened to do it would be like cutting off a limb from his body.

Now thoughts that had been in her own mind for some time came to the surface and she said tentatively:

"I have . . . something to . . . say to . . . you."

"What is it, my precious?" the Prince enquired.

He knew by her expression that she was worried. He drew her a little closer and waited for her to say what he had a feeling had to be said.

"If," Paulina began, "you have . . . changed your mind about . . . marrying me . . . I shall quite . . . understand."

The Prince started to reply, but she went on:

"I am . . . sure you can . . . explain your . . . absence in some way to the Tsar and make your . . . peace with . . . him."

"What would you feel if that is what I did?" the Prince asked.

"It would be . . . agony to . . . lose you," Paulina replied, "but even worse agony if I thought you had . . . given up so much for me and . . . regretted it."

"I told you I would have no regrets," the Prince answered. "Now that we have been together for these days alone and uninterrupted, I can only say that I love you a million times more than I did when we started our first dash for freedom."

There was no doubt of the sincerity in his voice, but Paulina felt she had to ask:

"Is that true . . . really . . . true?"

"I will convince you how true it is once you have my ring on your finger and you are completely and absolutely mine."

He did not wait for her answer but kissed her with burning, demanding kisses which made their hearts beat frantically and left them both breathless.

For Paulina it was her first awakening to passion.

The Prince felt her quiver in his arms, felt too a little flame on her lips which complemented the burning fire which consumed him.

After a moment he raised his head to say hoarsely:

"How can you doubt my love? How could you believe we could ever lose this miracle which has made us already, in the sight of God, one person?"

"I love you . . . you," Paulina whispered, "but you make me . . . feel so . . . strange, so . . . excited."

As she spoke she hid her face against his neck, and the Prince, conscious of the blood throbbing in his temples and his heart turning strange somersaults, said a little unsteadily:

"I have so much to teach you, my beautiful one, about love."

As he spoke he knew how very innocent and inexperienced she was and that he must be very gentle with her, awakening her slowly and gently to the raptures that he himself felt when he touched her.

Although Paulina was unaware of it, he had had to exercise an almost superhuman control of himself when with every passing mile they left farther and farther behind them the menacing hand of St. Petersburg.

Finding it impossible to sleep after he had kissed Paulina good-night, the Prince lay awake in the darkness, thinking of her, separated from her by only a heavy curtain, and longing for her with his whole body on fire.

It was only the discipline which had always been part of his life that prevented him from going to her.

He knew their marriage must be built not only on the firm foundation of trust and faith but on the idealism which he knew was so much a part of Paulina that he had sensed it from the first moment he had seen her.

There was something intrinsically pure about her, not only physically but spiritually, which made her different from every other woman the Prince had known.

It was a purity which protected her like an armour and kept him away as effectively as any locked door could have done.

"If I had a . . . choice," Paulina said in a very small voice, "I would like to . . . live with . . . you in a little hut where I could look after . . . you and show you how much my love . . . means."

"Wherever we live," the Prince replied, "either in a Palace or a little hut, it will be for both of us a secret place filled with love. And I will protect and shelter you all the years we are together."

Paulina gave a little sigh of happiness and then said:

"I am still . . . afraid what your father will . . . think, and if he will be very . . . angry."

"We will cross that bridge when we come to it," the Prince answered. "At the moment, all I want is to get you to safety and marry you. I have already decided where we will spend our honeymoon."

"A honeymoon!" Paulina exclaimed. "That is something I had not expected."

"It is what I want more than anything else in the world," the Prince said. "Then, my precious darling, I can tell you how much I love you and show you how much you mean to me."

"It sounds like . . . Heaven!" Paulina cried.

"It will be," the Prince promised.

* * *

In the morning when Paulina rose, she dressed quickly, choosing a plainer gown than the one she had worn when they boarded the train at St. Petersburg.

When she passed through the curtain to the other part of the coach, she found that the Prince was dressed in the full uniform of a Major-General.

He saw the question in her eyes, and before she asked it he explained:

"If by any terrible mischance the Tsar's men are waiting for us, my rank will at least ensure that we are treated with respect. If, on the other hand, all goes well, in Prussia a uniform is always to be obeyed."

"You look magnificent!"

"And you look very lovely," the Prince replied. "Kiss me good-morning, which is what I am waiting for."

Paulina flung her arms round his neck and he held her very close, looking down at her with such a loving expression in his eyes that she felt nothing mattered except themselves.

He kissed her until a bell ringing loudly on the front of the train warned them that they were approaching a station.

"Is . . . this the . . . border?" Paulina asked in a frightened voice.

"I think so," the Prince answered.

She drew in her breath and forced herself to sit down quietly on a seat.

The train drew to a standstill and they could see Russian officials standing on a rough, untidy platform.

She started praying.

"Please, God . . . help us. Please, God, do not let

us be . . . turned back. Please, God, do not let us be . . . captured at the . . . last moment."

Although the Prince said nothing, she knew he was tense.

When the officials came to the door of the coach, he stepped down to talk to them.

They looked strange in their elaborate uniforms which the Tsar had personally designed for them, which contrasted strongly with their rough-cut beards and their faces and hands, which needed washing.

There seemed to be a great deal of talk which inevitably in Russia went on and on.

If she had listened to it, Paulina would have found it hard to understand because it was a local dialect, but she did not attempt to do anything but pray.

She even shut her eyes for fear she would look up and see soldiers in uniform entering the coach.

Then when she felt that the tension which made it hard for her to breathe was almost suffocating her and she must either scream or faint, there was a sudden clash, a rumbling of wheels, ringing of bells, the noise of the engine letting off steam, and they were moving again.

She opened her eyes. She saw the Prince, felt his arms encircle her, and heard him exclaim in a note of triumph:

"We have won! We have won, my beloved! In a few moments we shall have left Russian soil forever."

The moment was so poignant and she had been so afraid that Paulina felt the tears running down her cheeks and she could only blindly lift her face to his.

He kissed her lips and then her tears away one by one.

A few moments later they came to a halt on the Prussian side of the border.

The efficiency of the station in Prussia was very different from the lethargy and incompetence so evident at the stations in Russia.

What was more, Paulina was aware that the Prince had been right in saying that his uniform would command attention.

Officials bowed to him obsequiously. There were porters to carry their luggage, and a comfortable and fast carriage was found with strong young horses.

Almost before Paulina could realise what was happening, they were driving over comparatively smooth roads between well-built houses with well-tended gardens which constituted the suburbs of the border town.

The sun seemed almost dazzling, and, feeling as if she had come from darkness into the light, Paulina asked:

"Where are we going now?"

"To have breakfast, I hope," the Prince replied. "You may feel as if you have already reached Paradise, my darling, and are disembodied with the rapture of it, but I am human and am feeling hungry."

Paulina laughed and said:

"Now that I think of it, so am I."

"I am sure we will find the food more palatable than what we had to endure on the train," the Prince answered.

Paulina laughed again.

What they had been provided with at the wayside stations had been rough and unappetising peasant food.

Fortunately there had been a number of pots of caviar in their coach left by the last occupant and owner, who would doubtless think when he travelled home from St. Petersburg that he had been robbed.

Paulina had been too happy most of the time even to notice the food.

Instead she had been quite content with the endless cups of tea from the samovar which was filled automatically at every stop and kept hot enough to drink until the next.

The Inn at which their carriage stopped was clean, and the moment they demanded breakfast, two apple-cheeked *Frauleins* with spotless aprons, their fair hair covered with well-starched caps, began to load the table with food.

"If we eat all this," Paulina whispered when the waitresses were out of the room, "we shall be like camels and be able to last unfed for days."

"I doubt it," the Prince answered. "At the same time, I am feeling more benign with every mouthful I swallow."

They drove on again and when they stopped for another meal it was more to give the horses a rest than because they themselves were hungry.

In the afternoon, Paulina realised that they were driving steadily up hill.

Ahead she could see mountains and guessed they were part of the great range which divided Altauss on the north and east from Saxony and Prussia.

Because she knew that the Prince wanted it to be a surprise, she did not ask questions but was content to hold his hand under the rug.

'This is how my whole life will be in the future,' she thought, 'in his hands, and I can imagine nothing more blissful.'

It was nearly six o'clock when a narrow bridge over a deep chasm carried them from Prussia into Altauss.

As the horses reached the ground on the other side, the Prince turned Paulina's face up to his:

"Welcome home, my precious, wonderful love," he said and kissed her.

Two minutes later they stopped in a village at the foot of a mountain.

It was little more than a hamlet, with only a few attractive white cottages, a small Church, and beside it a slightly larger house, outside which the horses came to a standstill.

"Wait for me," the Prince said.

Stepping down, he went to the door of a house. When it was opened he went inside.

Paulina knew where he had gone, and once again she was praying that everything would be as he wanted it to be.

He was away only a short time, and when he returned he was smiling as he said quietly but at the same time with a note of triumph in his voice:

"The Priest is waiting for us in the Church."

Paulina looked into his eyes. There was no need for words, for they both knew what the other was feeling without saying any more.

He helped her from the carriage and they walked up a rough path and in through the Church door.

The Church was very old and there was a fragrance of incense.

Paulina felt it was filled with the faith of those who had worshipped there over centuries of time.

The Priest waiting for them was an old man.

He spoke the words of the Marriage Service with sincerity and made it seem a ceremony and a sacrament that bound them together not only by the laws of man but by the blessing of God.

When their hands were joined and the Prince put a ring onto her finger, Paulina knew that it was a symbol of their love, and their union with each other would be for eternity.

"I love you," she wanted to say after every response, and those were the words the Prince said to her when finally they rose to their feet as man and wife.

"I love you," he said quietly.

He kissed first one of her hands and then the other, and she knew that she was the most blessed woman in the whole of the world.

Only as they drove on again together did Paulina ask:

"It is true . . . it is really true . . . that I am your wife? Even now I can hardly . . . believe it."

The Prince put his arm round her.

"I will make you believe it, Life of my Life, not only today but every day we are together."

"It is wonderful . . . so absolutely and completely wonderful . . ." Paulina cried. "Oh, Maximus, how can we be so fortunate that this should happen to us!"

"I thanked God for you when I was being married," the Prince answered, "and I will thank Him every day we live together for a happiness that could only have come from Him."

"How can you say such . . . wonderful things to me . . . and be so . . . different from any man I have ever known . . . before?" Paulina asked.

"Just as I ask myself how you can be so different from any other woman in the whole world," he replied. "I feel that to win you I have had to climb to the top of the highest mountain and dive down into the deepest depths of the sea. But I would do more, even storm Hell itself, rather than lose you!"

There was still quite a long way to go before finally on the side of the mountain Paulina saw a small but very attractive Castle and guessed that was where they were going.

She looked at the Prince enquiringly.

"This is where we will spend our honeymoon," he said.

Then after a pause he added:

"It is called Liedenburg Castle and it belongs to me. My father gave it to me as a Hunting Lodge when I was twenty-one. I love coming here, but I have always felt there was something missing—now I know it was you."

Paulina gave a little laugh of sheer happiness.

"Are you telling me that if we are ostracised for the way we have behaved and your father will not forgive you, this is where we will live?"

"Exactly," the Prince replied, "and I know, my dearest, I can make you happy."

"I would be happy wherever we were," Paulina

said. "But I want great things for you, and certainly not to make you give up what you have already for . . . me."

"We will talk about that another time," the Prince said. "All that concerns me at the moment is that you are my wife, and as a honeymoon is a time of love, everything else fades into insignificance."

When they reached the Castle, Paulina found that is was even more attractive inside than it had looked on the outside.

It was simply furnished but in perfect taste. The native rugs had been made by the women in the villages, and on the floor were also skins of wild animals that the Prince had shot himself.

The view from the windows was breathtaking.

There was a Baronial Hall, a small Dining-Room, a comfortable Sitting-Room, and a bedroom with a huge bed, locally carved and painted.

Everything Paulina saw made her exclaim with delight and admiration until she ran out of adjectives.

"I knew that you would like my house," the Prince said with a smile. "I chose everything myself. Wherever possible I used local craftsmen from the village, who are the best carvers in Altauss, and when I told them what I wanted they worked day and night to please me."

The result was so artistic and so original that Paulina felt it was like having an exquisite doll's-house to play with.

She loved the carved and painted furniture and the gilt frames of the pictures that hung on the walls. The curtains and hangings of the bedroom were, strangely enough, all in the blue that matched her eyes and was in fact her favourite colour.

"You might almost have chosen it as a background especially for me," she said.

"Perhaps fate was guiding me," the Prince answered, "and unconsciously I was reaching out towards you without realising it, because you were already in my heart."

He kissed her and left her to change from her travelling-clothes and have a bath.

There were two smiling young Altauss women to wait on Paulina, and she learnt from them that their parents had looked after the house for the Prince ever since he had owned it, and as they grew up the only thing they had wanted was to serve him too.

"We always hoped our Prince would marry some-one as lovely as Your Royal Highness!" one of them exclaimed.

When the girl addressed her formally, Paulina started. She had forgotten that as the Prince's wife they would expect her to be as Royal as he was.

She knew with a little throb of her heart that it was something she was not entitled to and that in conse-quence of his marriage he might lose this exalted rank.

However, there was nothing she could do about it at the moment, and she knew that to talk about it while they were on their honeymoon would worry and upset him.

"How can I ever make up to him for what he is risking for me?" she asked herself.

She knew there was only one way she could do so, and that was by loving him so completely and absolutely that he would never have any regrets.

When they dined together in the attractive Dining-Room, eating a delicious meal, simple but extremely well cooked, Paulina looked at the Prince sitting at the top of the table and thought how handsome he looked.

He wore the ordinary evening-clothes of a gentle-man and she was able to forget, for a moment, that he was a Prince and to think of him only as a man and her husband.

They were served a golden wine which came from the vineyards of Altauss. When dinner was over and the servants had left the room, the Prince raised his glass.

"To someone very beautiful, very brave, and my wife," he said softly.

"It was you who were brave," Paulina replied, "and I want to drink to the most wonderful man in the world, who is my . . . husband!"

Her lips just touched the glass, then the Prince pushed back his chair and drew her to her feet.

"You have had a long day, my darling," he said, "and now I am going to take you to bed."

Paulina did not answer, but as he took her hand in his, he was aware that her fingers were trembling.

They went upstairs to the bedroom, which was lit only by candles which threw a soft glow over the room.

The Prince shut the door behind him and then he said:

"Listen to me, my darling. Although you have never complained, I know exactly what you have been through these past days as we journeyed across Russia."

He put his arms round her as he went on:

"I can tell you how much I admire your courage in coming away with me and putting up with the discomforts of the journey, which we both know was beset by fear and anxiety."

"I . . . was with . . . you," Paulina whispered.

She moved closer into his arms and he kissed her forehead.

"Because of all that," the Prince went on, "if you would rather sleep in peace tonight, I shall understand."

Paulina raised her face to look up at him as he said:

"I want you, God knows how I want you, but because I love you, I know that to rush things might be a mistake."

Paulina knew no man could express his love more eloquently.

She was very innocent in that she did not know exactly what a man did when he made love to a woman, but she was aware that when the Prince kissed her he was excited.

When he had sent her to bed on the train, she knew it had been an effort for him not to go on kissing her and stay with her longer than he permitted himself to do.

She realised now that just as he was prepared to sacrifice his position in Russia and, what was much more, even his Throne in Altauss for love, so he was prepared to deny himself the rapture of their being together the first night of their marriage, if that was what she wished.

For the moment it was difficult to find the words in which to express what she felt, and then, hiding her face against his neck, she whispered:

"This is our ... wedding-night, and I want ... Maximus darling ... to be your ... wife."

* * *

Very much later, when the one candle they had left burning by the bed was guttering low, Paulina stirred in the Prince's arms.

He had drawn back the curtains, and lying against him she could see that the moonlight outside was touching the peaks of the mountains with silver, while over the valley below the great vista of sky was brilliant with stars.

Paulina turned her head so that her cheek was against the Prince's shoulder.

"When you first kissed me," she said, "I felt as if you carried me up to the ... stars, and now I know we are ... part of ... them. We are no ... longer on ... earth."

"That is what I feel too! Oh, my wonderful, perfect little wife, how could I ever have thought you were out of my reach?"

"I did not know ... love could be so ... wonderful."

"I have made you happy?"

"So very... very happy, and... you are not...
disappointed in... me?"

He gave a little laugh.

"How can you imagine I could be, when everything about you is perfect? A perfection which I thought
I would never find."

Paulina moved even closer to him as she said:

"You know I am very... ignorant about love, but
when you... made love to me I felt as if you... gave
me the sun... the stars, and the moon, and we were
both part of the Divine."

She paused for a moment and then went on:

"Was it the... same for you when you... made
love to... other... women?"

The Prince put his fingers under her chin and
turned her face up to his.

"I thought you might ask me that question, my
precious. Let me tell you as truly as if we were standing
in front of the altar, as we were this afternoon when we
were married, that the joy and rapture I felt with you is
different from anything I have ever known before."

He kissed her forehead before he went on:

"This is the love that I have always sought, which
is not only real but spiritual and sacred, and I swear I
have never known that with anyone else."

Paulina gave a little cry of happiness and then her
arms were round his neck, pulling his face down to
hers.

"I love you... I love you... how can I make you
understand I... love you! And how... happy I am... that
you love... me!"

"It is going to take at least a century to tell you
what I feel for you," the Prince said, "so we had better
start now telling each other of our love and hope we do
not run out of time."

"Even a... century is not long... enough for... me."

There was a note of passion in her voice that the
Prince knew had not been there before.

He thought she was like a flower opening to the
sun. Every day he would teach her more and more
about love and it would be the most fascinating and
exciting thing he had ever done.

He kissed her on her little arched eye-brows and
then on her eyes. He kissed the end of her nose,
knowing that her lips were ready and waiting for his.

"I love... you," Paulina said again breathlessly. "I
love you... and as I can... feel your... heart beating
against... mine... I know you... love me... too."

"Now you are deliberately exciting me," the Prince
said. "It is something you have not known how to do
before, my sweet one, but something you will undoubtedly do a great deal in the future."

"Is it... something I ought... not to... do?" she
asked childishly.

He laughed.

"It is something you will do whether you want to
or not. But it is very exciting for me that you wish to do
so, my darling. And it is something I will reciprocate
only too eagerly."

Then he was kissing her, kissing her fiercely,
demandingly, possessively.

She felt thrill after thrill run through her, like the
shafts of sunlight he had aroused in the past, only more
intense, more thrilling, and completely irresistible!

Once again he was carrying her up to the stars and
there was only him, his arms, his lips, his body, and his
love, and they were one.

*   *   *

It was three weeks later when they left the Castle
of Liedenburg and started the journey downhill to the
Palace of Wildenstadt.

Wearing her prettiest gown and her smartest bonnet, Paulina was very nervous and anxious about what
their reception would be.

She knew the Prince had written to his father,

telling him when they would be arriving and where they were staying on their honeymoon.

There had been no reply, and she was not certain whether it was because the Grand Duke wished to leave them in peace or whether he was too angry to communicate with them.

The Prince had anticipated that his father would return from Russia immediately after the wedding, but as he would be travelling the same way as he had arrived—by sea—it would take the best part of a week before he was back home.

"It will give him time to assimilate what has happened and doubtless discuss it with your father," he said to Paulina.

"Perhaps His Royal Highness will be so angry that he will send bad reports about Papa back to England," Paulina said unhappily.

"I am sure that is most unlikely," the Prince replied. "My father is above all things just, and he is also a sportsman. He would not inflict an unfair punishment on your father for a crime he had not committed."

"But . . . I am his . . . daughter."

"You are also my wife," the Prince replied.

He then pulled her into his arms and kissed her until she could no longer go on looking worried or anticipate what would be their reception when they finished their honeymoon and had to face the music.

Because every day was one of wild delight and an ecstasy beyond words, it was in fact very difficult to think of anything but her love for the Prince and his for her.

They rode down into the valley, where it was easy to gallop.

They climbed some way up the mountains.

Most of the time they were happy to sit in the beautiful gardens of the Castle and talk about themselves.

There was so much that Paulina wanted to know

about the Prince and so much he wanted to know about her.

There never seemed to be enough time to learn what they were eager to know, because once again he would be kissing her and then once again everything else was forgotten.

'Perhaps I am leaving my happiness behind... forever,' Paulina thought in a sudden panic as they drove away from the Castle.

Instinctively she moved a little nearer to her husband, and knowing what she was thinking he put his arms round her.

"Just remember," he said quietly, "we are married and nothing and nobody can separate us."

When she saw the Palace ahead, Paulina thought, as she always had, that it had a fairy-like quality and she loved it.

The sentries in their pink and white boxes saluted them and they drove up to the front door with a flourish.

Servants came hurrying down to greet the Prince.

There was no doubt that they were delighted to see him again and the smiles on their faces were those of welcome.

"His Royal Highness is expecting us, I think," the Prince said.

The Major-Domo in his best and most elaborate uniform led them pompously towards the Salon.

Because Paulina was frightened, she slipped her hand into the Prince's, unconcerned by what the servants might think and wanting only the comfort of touching him.

The Prince, however, seemed almost indifferent to whatever reproaches or reprimands were waiting for him.

Paulina knew it was because he was so happy and because in a way the last three weeks when they had been together had made him a different man.

She had known that when she married the Prince it was a rapture beyond words and a happiness that was impossible to express.

She had not expected it to be exactly the same for him, but yet it had been.

She knew—because she had seen her father and mother so happy together—that it was the same happiness that they had known and there was nothing in the world comparable to the treasure they possessed.

The Major-Domo flung open the door of the Salon.

He did not announce them and Paulina knew it was because he was not quite certain how he should address her or what her title might be.

'I am still only a commoner,' she thought to herself despairingly.

The Grand Duke was waiting for them at the far end of the room.

It seemed a long way as they walked towards him over the soft carpet. Paulina still clung to the Prince's hand and she felt that without it her feet might fail her and she would be unable to walk beside him.

They reached the Grand Duke.

"Good-afternoon, Father," the Prince said.

Paulina sank down in a deep curtsey. For the moment, because she was frightened, she dared not look at the Grand Duke's face, afraid of what she might see.

Then she rose, and she heard him say in quite genial terms:

"You two have caused a great deal of commotion!"

"I am sorry, Father," the Prince replied. "I would have warned you if I could, but I thought it best for you to be as ignorant of our intentions as everyone else."

Then, as if he could not control his curiosity, he asked:

"What happened when they learnt we had gone, and why?"

"I thought you would want the answer to that

question," the Grand Duke said. "Perhaps you had better sit down while I tell you what occurred."

Tentatively Paulina sat down on the edge of a sofa and the Prince sat beside her.

The Grand Duke, in a high-backed armchair opposite them, seemed, she thought hopefully, quite at ease.

They waited, and after a moment the Grand Duke said:

"You timed your departure cleverly. It was only after Margarita's wedding that the Tsar began to make enquiries as to where you were."

"Did anyone know the answer?" the Prince enquired.

"No. Not until Benckendorff's spies were sent scurrying in all directions to search for you and learnt that you had boarded a train, accompanied by a young woman."

"About what time was that?" the Prince enquired.

"About the middle of the afternoon," the Grand Duke answered. "By then Margarita had asked— unfortunately in the Tsar's hearing—what had happened to her Lady-in-Waiting."

The Grand Duke's eyes were twinkling as he went on:

"Someone suggested—I imagine to smooth over an awkward moment—that she might have left for the Palace where the young couple were to start their honeymoon. But of course later the Tsar put two and two together."

"Was he angry?" the Prince enquired.

"Furious, insulted, and enraged, are better words," the Grand Duke replied. "He threw an Imperial tantrum, and having told me in no uncertain terms what he thought of my son, he stripped you of your rank and kicked you out of the Russian Army."

Paulina gave a little cry of horror, but the Prince merely smiled as he said:

"It was what I expected."

There was silence.

Then in a low voice he added:

"All the same, I shall miss being a soldier."

"You appear to have forgotten that we have an Army of our own," the Grand Duke remarked drily. "Not so large or so aggressive, but I think in the troublesome times in which we live it should be built up and modernised."

There was a light in the Prince's eyes as he asked:

"You mean that, Father?"

"I think it would be a mistake for you to lose your military rank," the Grand Duke replied.

The Prince gave a smile and it was as if sunlight filled the room.

Then he said:

"As I told you in my note, Paulina and I are married."

"In a somewhat hole-in-the-corner manner," the Grand Duke remarked.

"Nevertheless, it is completely and absolutely binding," the Prince replied.

It was as if they fenced with each other, and Paulina held her breath.

Then the Grand Duke said:

"You realise that under the laws of Altauss, your marriage is a morganatic one."

"That I accept," the Prince said, "but as I have already said, it is completely and absolutely binding."

There was a frightening silence before the Grand Duke replied:

"In which case your wife has to have a name."

"Yes, Father."

"I have been giving it my consideration," the Grand Duke went on slowly, "and I find there is an unused title belonging to the Castle where you spent your honeymoon."

Paulina felt it hard to breathe, and she clenched her fingers together in her lap.

"I therefore propose," the Grand Duke continued,

"to give your wife, Maximus, the title of Her Serene Highness Princess Paulina of Liedenburg."

The Prince opened his lips to speak, but the Grand Duke finished:

"When she has been accepted by our people as the right sort of wife for the Ruler of our country, and when you take my place, it will be up to you to make her and your children Royal in the full sense of the word."

The Prince gave a shout which seemed to echo round the room.

"Father, you are a sportsman!" he exclaimed. "How can I thank you? How can I tell you what this means to me and to Paulina?"

"I want you to be happy, my son," the Grand Duke said simply.

The Prince shook his father's hand, and Paulina rose with tears of happiness in her eyes to stand beside him.

The Grand Duke kissed her cheek.

"Welcome, my new daughter-in-law," he said. "Now we will send for your father, who is waiting to welcome you both."

*   *   *

That night there was a dinner-party at which the Grand Duke and Sir Christopher drank the health of the young couple, joined by numerous relatives who seemed to appear from nowhere.

Even before they left, the Prince and his wife—Her Serene Highness—had retired to their bedroom in the Palace.

It was a large and very impressive State-Room, but Paulina thought it was not half as beautiful as their room in the Castle.

Yet, at the moment she could only look at her husband with love in her eyes, feeling in her heart an irrepressible gratitude not only to the Grand Duke but to God.

As he shut the door behind them she ran into his arms.

Looking down at her radiant face turned to his, he asked:

"Are you happy, my darling?"

"How can I be anything else when everything is so marvellous?" she replied. "I was so afraid... so desperately afraid that your father would be angry and I should not only have spoilt your relationship with him, but your... life in Altauss."

"I think we have given both my father and yours a new interest in life," he answered. "They will doubtless compete for the affection of their grandchildren, which will mean they will be spoilt to death."

He watched the colour come into Paulina's cheeks and loved the shyness in her eyes.

She hid her face against his shoulder as she said:

"I want to... give you a... son. But I was so ... afraid he might not be allowed to inherit your ... position, and that would make you... unhappy."

"I think you would have been more unhappy about it than I was," the Prince said. "Instead, it is a problem we can forget. Just as we can forget Russia and the Tsar's anger."

As he spoke he knew that Paulina was still a little distressed that he had lost the decorations he had won in battle.

"I have no regrets," he said softly.

She smiled up at him.

"One lesson," he went on, "we have both learnt from this."

"What is... that?"

He pulled her still closer to him and his lips moved over the softness of her skin as he answered:

"The affection of Monarchs is fickle and unreliable, and only when love rules is there lasting happiness."

"As it does for us, darling, wonderful Maximus, and... nothing shall take our happiness from us."

As Paulina spoke she pressed her lips against her husband's.

He pulled her almost roughly against him, and the fire which burnt only a little way beneath the surface burst into flame.

He kissed her passionately and fiercely, as if demanding that she surrender herself to him.

She was not afraid; she knew this was the burning heat of the sun that was also a part of their lives.

As it consumed them both, the stars came nearer and nearer until as Maximus carried her to bed they were with them and in them, and ruled over by Love.

Barbara Cartland is the bestselling author in the world, according to the *Guinness Book of Records*. She has sold over 200 million books and has beaten the world record for five years running, last year with 24 and the previous years with 24, 20, and 23.

She is also an historian, playwright, lecturer, political speaker and television personality, and has now written over 320 books.

She has also had many historical works published and has written four autobiographies as well as the biographies of her mother and that of her brother, Ronald Cartland, who was the first Member of Parliament to be killed in the last war. This book has a preface by Sir Winston Churchill and has just been republished with an introduction by Sir Arthur Bryant.

Love at the Helm, a novel written with the help and inspiration of the late Earl Mountbatten of Burman, uncle of His Royal Highness Prince Philip, is being sold for the Mountbatten Memorial Trust.

Miss Cartland, in 1978, sang an Album of Love Songs with the Royal Philharmonic Orchestra.

She is unique in that she was #1 and #2 in the Dalton List of Bestsellers, and one week had four books in the top twenty.

In private life Barbara Cartland, who is a Dame of the Order of St. John of Jerusalem, Chairman of the St. John Council in Hertfordshire and Deputy President of the St. John Ambulance Brigade, has also fought for better conditions and salaries for midwives and nurses.

As President of the Royal College of Midwives (Hertfordshire Branch) she has been invested with the first badge of Office ever given in Great Britain, which was subscribed to by the Midwives themselves.

Barbara Cartland is deeply interested in vitamin therapy and is President of the British National Association for Health. Her book, *The Magic of Honey*, has sold through the world and is translated into many languages.

She has a magazine "Barbara Cartland's World of Romance" now being published in the U.S.A.